A. Shane Bishop

IDOL
THREAT

WRITTEN BY
BRYCE ALLEN

FIRST TRADE PAPERBACK EDITION

IDOL THREAT
© 2018 by Bryce Allen
Cover art © 2018 by Matthew Revert

This edition © 2018 Bedlam Press

ISBN: 978-1-944703-59-2
LOC: 2018942669

Assistant Editors:
C. Dennis Moore

Special Thanks to Robert Funkhouser

Book design & typesetting:
David G. Barnett
Fat Cat Graphic Design
www.fatcatgraphicdesign.com

Bedlam Press
an imprint of
Necro Publications
5139 Maxon Terrace
Sanford, FL 32771
www.necropublications.com

10 9 8 7 6 5 4 3 2 1

IDOL THREAT

BEDLAM PRESS

— 2018 —

PROLOGUE

A veneer of civility had vanished, the scene's score dropping a full octave into a much more menacing register.

Declan Farrelly's expression had likewise transformed. His searing emerald eyes now glared through Bulakin with unbridled ferocity. "What did you say? How much??" Farrelly's firmly-clenched jaw jutted outwards, aggressively.

"One. Hundred. Thousand." Bulakin stated, returning his counterpart's intense gaze. After an incredibly-anxious moment spent staring forcefully into Declan's stolid mask of a face he added, wryly: "You are not happy with this new price I take it?"

"It's double what we'd agreed upon," Declan snarled. "What do you take me for? An idiot? Some kind of amateur??"

"Not at all." Bulakin's placidity was remarkable. The corpulent underworld figure was clearly quite used to dealing with volatile situations such as these. He radiated nothing but smug professionalism as he smiled knowingly and slowly, prudently removed a smoldering cigarette butt from between his thick, leathery lips and tossed it haphazardly to the arid soil.

"My company is merely adjusting its business model to accommodate recent changes in the global marketplace. These adjustments are including the increasing of the mark-up on certain products, including Russian-made PFM-1 and PTM-1 land mines."

The blood surging through Declan's veins grew hotter with every syllable Bulakin spat forth. *Who does this Eurotrash gorilla think he's dealing with?*

"We have been doing business together for many months now," Bulakin continued, his Kiev-meets-Krakow accent sounding utterly preposterous, as if he were a bad actor playing the villain in a Cold War-era spy film. "You have been a good customer. You are always placing the next order before we deliver a shipment. But not this time. There is no order after this one. I am sensing that this will be our final business transaction together."

"So, you thought you'd make a few extra bucks on this one then, eh Vladimir?" Declan's sharp, soldier's eyes quickly scanned the area for any signs of danger before he made his next move. A moonless night had blanketed their usual meeting place in oppressive darkness. The ragged terrain which stretched out for acres around them revealed nothing, the barren horizon a tenebrous abyss.

Sensing no threat, Declan sighed expressively, returning his focus to the loathsome arms dealer standing before him. Bulakin's long, greasy black hair dangled limply over a grotesque, reptilian face which quite obviously belonged to one of the most dangerous men on the planet.

Declan had met with Bulakin several times over the course of the preceding year, always at the same remote location and always with just the two of them completing the weapons-for-cash exchange. Now, the gluttonous criminal he'd handed nearly two million dollars over to during their fleeting association had decided to change things up, to play some kind of exigent game with his best customer. Declan had no choice but to play along.

"Look, Vlad, all I brought with me was the fifty grand we agreed upon. See for yourself." Declan tossed a duffle bag at the

Ukrainian gangster, reaching into his jacket pocket and pulling out a CZ-75 semi-automatic pistol as soon as the cash-filled satchel left his hands.

Bulakin instinctively grabbed the bag out of mid-air, momentarily distracted. Declan exploited the impromptu diversion to full effect, immediately aiming his gun squarely at the death-merchant's thick forehead. "So, if you could simply take my money and give me my merchandise, I'll be on my way."

He had the upper hand. The game was over.

Bulakin jostled the canvas sack gently, confirming that it indeed contained a significant amount of cash. "I will be glad to take your money, Irishman. I would also like to keep my merchandise however." He began to chuckle to himself gruffly as Declan cocked his wrist, gripping his gun's handle tightly as a badly-calloused index finger fondled its trigger.

"What's so funny?" Is this some kind of sick joke to you? I'll kill you right now if you don't shut up!" As soon as the words left his mouth he could hear it. A gentle rustling was now faintly audible behind him, the muted theme music of an advancing enemy contingent.

Bulakin's chuckle quickly escalated into an all-out guffaw. "I believe in English the expression is 'here comes the cavalry', yes?"

With lightning-fast speed Declan lunged forward and grabbed Bulakin by the throat, the obese outlaw's torpid reflexes betraying him as his beefy arms flailed about futilely while his assailant's grip tightened with astonishing strength. A sickening gurgling sound accompanied the crushing of Bulakin's windpipe, Declan's powerful fingers tearing through flesh as if it were paper maché, blood surging out of the fresh wounds like a raging geyser. Unmitigated terror quickly filled the foreign gunrunner's eyes.

A crimson shower bombarding him, Declan pulled his colossal victim forward. Using every ounce of strength he could muster, the one-time rugby prodigy managed to keep Bulakin's dying body from keeling over as he forcibly switched positions with the three-hundred-pound corpse-to-be.

Bulakin's wide backside now faced his advancing henchmen as the life faded from his dark, beady eyes. "Teper! Teper!!" Declan shouted in a semi-believable Ukrainian twang. *Now! Now!!*

Almost immediately a deafening chorus of gunfire ripped through the sultry summer air. A quintet of silhouetted figures suddenly became vaguely visible in the vibrant glow produced by a series of fleeting orange-tinged flashes, discharged from the barrels of five identical Vepr assault rifles.

Bulakin's ample frame absorbed dozens of bullets as the gunmen continued to fire for several seconds before realizing what they'd done. "Khrin," one of them said, plainly.

With his generously-sized human shield in tow, Declan advanced upon his attackers as soon as they stopped shooting. Relinquishing his grasp of Bulakin's trachea, Declan crouched into a baseball catcher's stance as the massive body staggered backwards. He fired several rounds into the darkness as Bulakin collapsed upon the impotent California farmland, the resulting *thud* nearly matching Declan's pistol in volume.

Two distinct cries of agony were audible amidst a calamity of Ukrainian curse words and retaliatory gunfire. *Three to go.*

Exhibiting Olympic-caliber agility Declan retrieved his duffle bag and leapt upon the back of Bulakin's pickup truck, immediately ducking behind the large metallic crate its cargo bed housed. As gunfire continued to assail him, Declan frantically searched for a crowbar with his left hand as he blindly fired his handgun over the fully-stocked container with his right.

Upon finding the curved metallic bar Declan quickly jimmied open the crate, removing one of the mines just as one bullet nicked his arm and another shattered the truck's rear window.

Dangerously tossing the mine through the fractured window, onto the passenger seat, Declan swiftly crawled into the cabin. Broken glass sliced through his thin silk shirt and cut into his stomach, causing the Dubliner to wince in pain. Another gunshot grazed his left shoulder and proceeded to blast through the truck's windshield. Declan managed to force himself into the driver's seat, a six-cylinder engine springing to life almost immediately. "Thanks for leaving the keys in the ignition, Vladimir," Bulakin's final customer muttered to himself

After shifting into first gear Declan grabbed the deadly green device sitting next to him. He removed its arming pin and dropped it out of the open passenger window.

Declan looked in the driver's side mirror to see three poorly-illuminated figures sprinting towards him, their guns still blazing as a crevice of moonlight now beamed down upon the vacant lot. A bullet ricocheted off the front left tire's oversized rim just as Declan shifted into second gear, the American-made vehicle now humming with urgency.

An ear-splitting explosion erupted seconds later as one of Bulakin's henchmen stepped upon the active mine Declan had left behind. His body blew apart in a fountain of blood and limbs as the remaining would-be-assassins immediately ceased their pursuit of their boss' killer, a bright ball of fire rocketing upwards into the dense, black sky.

Declan exhaled loudly as he again shifted up a gear, the powerful truck now approaching 50 MPH as it leapt onto a gravel road. He was already furious with himself for having been unprepared for such a poorly-designed ambush. *You're starting to slip, old man.*

An encroaching, eerie silence was extinguished by the tinny bleeps of a custom ringtone. Declan hurriedly retrieved his cell phone and pressed it to his thin, finely-drawn mouth.

"Hello?" Declan groaned into the receiver, his aging body now aching badly.

"How did it go?" a raspy, dissonant voice on the other end of the expertly-sterilized line inquired.

"I've got some good news," Declan said playfully, steering the speeding truck with an elbow as he picked shards of glass out of his midsection. "I got us a discount on the shipment. One hundred percent off."

"Excellent," the voice replied, excitedly. "That's everything then. Our arsenal is fully stocked. Operation Tacticus may now proceed to Phase Two. The United States of America... shall soon be no more."

《《《———》》》

I remove a jar of peanut butter from the cupboard. I unscrew the lid and place the jar on the counter next to a pre-sliced loaf of bread. I retrieve a butter knife from the cutlery drawer and jam the non-serrated blade right into the delicious food paste derived primarily from dry roasted peanuts. I pull a single slice of bread from the loaf with my left hand and remove the aforementioned butter knife from the aforementioned jar with my right, scooping out a small amount of creamy goodness as I do so. I gently press the knife against the bread slice and spread the peanut butter around until the surface is sufficiently covered. I rinse the knife off in my sink and place it in my dishwasher. I retrieve a fresh, clean knife from the cutlery drawer as well as another slice of bread from the loaf. I open my refrigerator door and locate a jar of raspberry jelly using my eyes – handy little organs that convert light into images via a complex system of neural pathways and such. I grab this new jar and place it on the counter next to the slice I've already applied peanut butter upon. A tiny dragon flies through the kitchen window and starts attacking me so I slay the thing with a steak knife after shielding myself from its fire-breath with a cheap aluminum tray. I dispose of the mini-dragon's carcass via the garbage disposal and then insert the bulbous end of my butter knife into the jelly jar and scoop out a small amount of jelly. I spread the jelly onto the blank slice of bread and place the knife into my sink, where it shall await to be properly cleaned until my hunger hath been quenched. I put the two pieces of bread together and sink my teeth into the most delicious fucking PB & J sandwich ever created.

I'm sitting at a table at some shitty café on the outskirts of Moscow waiting for some asshole that wants to hire me for a job up in St. Petersburg to show up. Oh yeah—FYI, I got back into the 'private security' game after a brief, boring retirement here in Russia. Luckily it turns out my services are in high demand in this part of the world thanks to all the shady shit that goes on over here and what not. So that's good.

"More tea, sir?" this frumpy, middle-aged waitress asks me, an edge of hostility in her voice. I've been sitting here for almost an hour waiting on this prick to arrive and I guess she's getting tired of me getting my dainty little tea cup filled every few minutes but hey, I'm a customer for fuck's sake so to hell with her, right?

I check my smartphone and the guy still hasn't called or texted me yet and I'm sick of the awful tea this place has so I let the bitch off the hook and tell her to just get my check. She shoots me a cockeyed glance and tells me the bill's a hundred rubles, so I leave her 101 just to be a dick.

After helping myself to a handful of mints from the café's counter and shoving them in my jacket pocket I leave my agent a voicemail telling him that the jerk he set me up with never showed and that I'm going to do some shopping at the local market now. "You don't really need to know that last part, but I'm wasting your time just like your stupid contact wasted mine," I add. Then I recite the lyrics to 'American Pie' in English until an electronic beep cuts me off and ends my message. So, I call back and recite the next couple of verses until I get bored with the whole thing, which is bound to happen in situations such as these.

Most of the kiosks at the market I frequent are peddling cheap trinkets, shoddy electronics and second-rate Western-style clothing but a small, rinky-dink little store I haven't noticed before catches my eye for some reason so I step inside the ancient-looking shop and look around.

"Welcome," the geriatric shopkeeper says to me, limping out from behind the counter with the help of a makeshift cane that looks like it was fashioned out of a fallen tree branch by a shitty woodworker. This old clerk looks like something straight out of a comic book about wizards—long, grey beard; antique glasses; greasy, disheveled hair; brown, uneven teeth… he's even wearing a goddamn purple robe for Christ's sake. "How can I help you?" he asks. His breath is spearmintergreen fresh, which is a pleasant surprise.

"Just browsing," I say, taking inventory of the store's... inventory. It's mostly antique knickknacks and junk, some hardcover books and a few odds and ends. Nothing special. "Got anything in here worth buying, old-timer?"

"Oh, most certainly," the shopkeeper sneers. "What are you looking for exactly?"

"Anything really. Or nothing. I don't know, I just wandered in here—not sure why." I grab a half-filled mason jar from one of the shelves and the shopkeeper snatches it from my hand. "That's a highly-potent metamorphosis potion!" He places it back on the shelf with the utmost of care. "It shouldn't even be on display come to think of it. How silly of me."

"Whatever, pops." I take a walk down an aisle and the old man is right on my tail the whole time. He *seems* harmless, but you never know; he could be a total psycho. I make it to a row of dust-covered books that all look like they're about a thousand years old. I examine the titles and they're all about weird occult stuff which kinda creeps me out but not really.

"You have anything more recent?" I ask. "Like from this century? Or the last one, that was pretty good too."

The shopkeeper flashes a devious smile at me and nods. "I do indeed. What type of book did you have in mind?"

"Well, to be honest, I haven't really been much of a reader since I was a kid." I rack my brain, trying to think of the last book I even read, and can't. Damn. No wonder I sucked at retirement. And school. And life. "I used to love those choose-your-own-adventure books back in grade school. You got any of those?"

The shopkeeper looks confused, so I explain to him that I grew up in the United States. That particular book franchise must not have made it over here I guess, which makes sense since that was back when the commies were running things and they probably didn't like the concept of 'choosing'... or 'adventures'... #Politics.

Old Man Река goes ahead and asks me what brought me to Russia, so I explain it to him. We stand there for like an hour as I tell the guy my tale and the bastard doesn't even blink an eye even though most of what I tell him is batshit crazy stuff[1]. I haven't really told anyone the full story since it all went down so it feels pretty good to get it all off my chest to be honest.

"And now fate has brought you here to my humble shop on this lovely day, yes?"

"I guess so. Fate is a virginal slut though if you ask me. Or a slutty virgin. Either way."

"Alright... And you've just now decided to become a reader after all of this time?"

"Apparently. I've got a lot of free time to kill nowadays, especially since a job I was supposed to get just fell through."

"And you enjoy books in which you're able to dictate the course of action the characters take? This is what a 'choose-your-own-adventure' book is I take it?"

"Pretty much, dude. Doesn't look like what you've got will suit me though—never even heard of any of these books." I issue a formal, dismissive wave towards his collection of leather-bound compendiums and the guy glowers at me pretty harshly.

"I can assure you that this is one of the finest collections of its kind in Europe—perhaps the world," he says, proudly.

"I'm sure it is, gramps, I'm sure... Just ain't my cup of tea I guess." I start to leave the store, but the old man grabs my arm, so I stop.

"Don't be so hasty," he says, assertively. "I believe I have just what you're looking for in the back room."

---

[1] Allen, Bryce, *The Spartak Trigger*, ASIN: B00J27G8PI; Bedlam Press (An Imprint of Necro Publications), 2014

"So, go get it then," I tell him. Fuckin' guy.

The shopkeeper retreats to the back room and I look around a little more. Next to the book section is a bunch of shrunken heads and shit which is pretty goddamn weird I don't mind saying. Next to the shrunken heads is more bizarro wizard junk and just when I think about making a run for it the old man appears in a flash of light right next to me and hands me a computer tablet. Looks kinda like a zPad.

"Thanks." I take the tablet and inspect it like a... guy who inspects things. You know what I mean. "This a new model?"

"It's one of a kind," the old man tells me. "A magical device, to be sure."

"I've seen their ad campaign too, Gandolf, I've heard the taglines... What's so special about this one?"

"Let's just say it's been customized with extra powers... Also, it has a pre-loaded program installed which is quite similar to the type of book you're looking for. I believe the program is called 'LiveStory'—you simply type in the basic elements of what you'd like to have happen and the computer turns it into a novel for you to enjoy."

"That sounds like a lot of work, friendo. I just wanted to pick what the main guy does at the end of a chapter or whatever."

"Well I think you'll find this much more engaging and entertaining," the shopkeeper says. "Shall I ring it up for you?"

"Yeah, sure. I'll give it a whirl. Plus, I can get my email and shit on this thing, right?"

The shopkeeper nods and makes his way over to the counter. "Cash or credit?" he asks.

"Credit." I hand him the pre-loaded credit card my former employer gave me that I've been living off of for over a year now and he takes an imprint on it on one of those old school flatbed thingies that no one's seen in forever. "Is there anything else I can do for you, good sir?" the shopkeeper asks after handing me back my credit card and a copy of the charge clip.

"You have any mogwais or gremlins I can buy?" I ask.

The old man doesn't get the reference and looks at me like I'm crazy, so I just grab the tablet and storm out of the place.

《《《—》》》

I drive home to Tula (Russian: Тула) and fire up my brand spanking new computer tablet as soon as I get situated in my tiny, Soviet/minimalist-style apartment. It's been a few weeks since I checked my email, so I log onto my TMail account and skim through the dozens of messages I've accumulated during my lengthy online hiatus.

The first message I get is from the deposed monarch of some country called 'Rodinia' asking for me to send him some money to help him pay the processing fee to retrieve his frozen assets from the national bank that was recently captured by the rebel army, so he can buy his way back into power somehow. He seems like a nice guy and the email is really well-written, so I wire him a grand and wish him well.

Email No. 2 is from some company trying to sell me a pill to help with my erectile dysfunction. I write them back and tell them my wang is just fine and dandy but thanks for the offer.

The third nouveau communiqué I read is from some dude named Robert Anderson and has my daughter's name— 'IRIS BISHOP' —in all-caps as its subject heading, which means that it's important. I skim the message and it turns out this Anderson guy is a Hollywood agent who'd recently signed Iris as a client. Interesting. I vaguely remember her acting in some fruity play back when she was in high school but that may have been a dream or a drug-induced hallucination or a REKAL implant or a fragment from some kind of collective memory pool the psychic overlords have created for us... Impossible to tell really.

So, anyway, according to Anderson's email, Iris has been missing for almost a week and he's filed a police report and shit, but the cops haven't managed to come up with anything yet, so he felt obligated to inform me, her only living family member, of her disappearance. Thoughtful gesture.

The whole thing sounds fishy as hell, so I write Anderson back and tell him I'll be on a flight to California soon and I'll be in contact once I'm back in the States. Then I book an expensive fucking plane ticket from Moscow to LAX for tomorrow afternoon. The arrest warrant for me was expunged a few months back after everything got sorted out back home so I'm all good to travel overseas again[2]. I just haven't yet because... I haven't. Yeah.

I'm curious about that choose-your-own-adventure book program the wizard-looking cat from the shop told me about so I open it up after I'm done making travel plans and my inbox is sufficiently tended to. LiveStory's artwork is annoyingly flashy but the program's not too tough to navigate.

A cartoon typeface asks me what kind of book I want it to write and I tell it to make something with Nazis since they make the best bad guys. Hands down. It asks me to specify so I type in 'use that evil dude Himmler who wanted to find the Ark of the

---

[2] Exposition [ek-spuh-zish-uh n], noun.
A large-scale public exhibition or show, as of art or manufactured products: an exposition of 19th-century paintings; an automobile exposition.
The act of expounding, setting forth, or explaining: the exposition of a point of view.
Writing or speech primarily intended to convey information or to explain; a detailed statement or explanation; explanatory treatise: The students prepared expositions on familiar essay topics.

Covenant and the Holy Grail to take over the world in those fedora-archeologist-guy movies... have the guy actually find something like that first though and make it cool and shit, Computer'.

The program takes forever to process the opening chapter and when it's finally done I start reading...

CHAPTER I

REINHARD KRAUSS stared keenly upon his poorly-bandaged left hand, wondering if the wound might have somehow become infected during the ceremony, or perhaps during the three days he had since spent negotiating the rugged terrain of Paderborn's countryside.

Exhausted from an arduous, sleepless journey and from years spent mired in a seemingly endless mode of combat, Krauss now sat in perplexed silence somewhere along the Alme River, pondering the least-dangerous route he might take back to his hometown of Bakum. At that moment, his beloved village in Lower Saxony seemed thousands of lifetimes away.

Steaming, lilting mist delicately caressed the passive river flowing before him—a rare scene of tranquility in a country besieged by hatred and ravaged with bloodshed... Momentarily overtaken by an unfamiliar, unnerving sense of serenity, Krauss breathed in deeply, his sense of vigor slowly returning. He stood slowly, his mind again focused solely upon the task at hand as he pressed on towards a destiny burdened with obstacle.

Since abandoning Wewelsburg Castle seventy-odd hours earlier, the burly, barrel-chested SS Officer had come within striking distance of no fewer than five Allied convoys, managing to elude them all in dramatic fashion. His colleagues had not been as fortunate as he however, and eleven corpses, each with an identical, self-inflicted gash upon their left palm now lay strewn across the Western front, awaiting an undeservedly ignoble burial. As the last surviving constituent of the Knights of the Order of the Black Sun, the burden of fulfilling the blood oath sworn to their master was now placed solely upon Reinhard Krauss, Heinrich Himmler's favorite disciple.

Years earlier, Himmler had magnanimously rescued Krauss, a carpenter by trade, from the bottomless pit of mordant obscurity, recruiting him for training in an SS cadet program during a chance tour through the German countryside. The Reichsführer had dutifully guided the impressionable, talented young soldier all the way to the rank of Obergruppenführer, knighted him upon the declaration of war with Poland, and had ordained his newborn sons by marking their foreheads with the sacred, ethereal mark of the Black Sun—the highest laurel Krauss could possibly imagine. Now, the Order's destiny lay entirely in Krauss' hands and he was possessed with an unbridled determination to survive the war, escape Europe, and honor his oath at any cost.

For years, Himmler and his loyal band of SS Knights had worked tirelessly in outlining the dogmatic principles from which a new Germanic religion would be forged—a faith steeped in the Nordic traditions and which drew extensively upon various mystical elements from all of the world's great historical empires. Not even the Führer himself had known of these plans, as they were never discussed outside of Wewelsburg's walls.

Christianity, Himmler had stated time and time again, was the most ingenious ploy ever conceived by the Jews in their quest to subjugate the Aryan race—a despicable religion forged upon inadequacy, guilt, and a sense of overbearing humility which trapped its practitioners in a web of self-loathing and fear, making them unable to fulfill the immense potential of the human spirit. While Jesus had indeed been the son of God, his teachings had been perverted over the years and evolved into a gross misrepresentation of the Creator's wishes for mankind, all at the hands of the Elders of Zion. Once the war was won, the Order of the Black Sun would reign supreme as the forbearers of the greatest, most awe-inspiring theology the world had ever known—a sanctimonious faith worthy of the Reich and its citizenry.

There would be no victory for Germany however, a fact that was now painfully obvious. As a result, a divergent path to glory had hastily been assembled, with Krauss and his brethren set to carry on with the Order's plans abroad.

The last reports Krauss had heard from the East proclaimed the Soviets to be on the outskirts of the capital, knocking loudly upon the doors of triumph. Hitler was now confined at all times to the bunker he had built beneath the once glorious center of Berlin—a site that was to have served as the functional heart of the Reich for the next thousand years.

Krauss had once visited the Reich Chancellery in the early days of the war, accompanying Himmler on what had been a pleasant, hospitable stay in which much laughter was shared and many plans for the future glories of the Aryan race were made. The cinematic image of crumbling, ruinous buildings littered throughout Germany's greatest city now instilled simultaneous feelings of hate and sorrow within Krauss' perilous psyche[3].

Time to spend mourning his nation's military defeat was not a luxury the devoted National Socialist could afford however.

---

[3] From Wikipedia: 'Show, don't tell' is a technique often employed in various kinds of texts to enable the reader to experience the story through action, words, thoughts, senses, and feelings rather than through the author's exposition, summarization, and description. The goal is not to drown the reader in heavy-handed adjectives, but rather to allow readers to interpret significant details in the text....

Within a week's time, Krauss had successfully made his way back to Bakum, reuniting with his infant sons Heinrich and Wolfgang. Fraternal twins whose health had benefited greatly from experimental serums concocted by renowned chemical eugenicist Dr. Karl Genzken, Reinhard's offspring had been left in the care of a trustworthy wet nurse following his wife Helga's untimely death the previous summer[4].

In addition to his young sons, from Bakum Reinhard retrieved the artifact Himmler had entrusted him with shortly after Germany's loss became inevitable… The Spear of Destiny, the Holy Lance that had pierced Jesus' side as he was strung up upon the cross. A few weeks prior to the declaration of war with Poland it had been obtained by the Ahnenerbe during an archaeological expedition in northern Italy. Now it belonged to Krauss, its divine powers likewise in his possession.

Himmler had kept the spear a secret from Hitler, waiting for the perfect time to use it to seize leadership of the party and reign supreme over the Reich. As it turned out, he'd waited too long and soon the Reichsführer-SS would be dead along with the rest of his Order. Reinhard Krauss was the fraternity's only hope, the lone knight capable of fulfilling its destiny.

Under cover of night, Krauss and his infant boys abandoned Bakum. The young family surrendered to the first English-speaking battalion they came across while posing as simple refugees anxious for sanctuary after having fled his now Soviet-occupied village of Vichtenstein.

---

[4] From Wikipedia: A 'note' is a string of text placed at the bottom of a page in a book or document or at the end of a chapter, volume or the whole text. The note can provide an author's comments on the main text or citations of a reference work in support of the text, or both. In English, a footnote is normally flagged by a superscripted number immediately following that portion of the text the note is in reference to, each such footnote being numbered sequentially. At times, notes have been used for their comical effect, or as a literary device :)

An expert in both governmental forgery and bureaucratic manipulation, Krauss had little trouble falsifying a foreign passport and assuming the identity of Reinhard Fuerst—a cowardly absconder from an Austrian Feldgendarmerie battalion. With a new surname in tow, he and his sons were permitted refuge in Sicily where they quickly boarded a cargo ship bound for the United States. Aside from the well-hidden spear they carried with them but a few meager belongings along with the final remnants of the Order of the Black Sun—a set of guidelines and rituals deeply ingrained within Krauss' consciousness.

Ensuring the formation of a Fourth Reich upon American soil was now Reinhard's sole function in life. It was the greatest mission in human history, one he intended to fulfill at any cost.

«««—»»»

Domodedovo International Airport is insanely busy tonight. There's a bunch of snot-nosed little Ruskie kids running around screaming their lungs off for no fucking reason and their parents don't give a damn so I start telling them I'm a secret agent from the North Pole spying on kids for Santa Claus, but they don't seem to understand what the fuck I'm talking about. At any rate, the confusion shuts them up, so mission accomplished I guess.

I get on the plane and fire up my tablet. The LiveStory program is already running which is weird since I shut it down after I'd used it before but whatever. My tablet asks me if Chapter I was 'satisfactory' and I type in 'yes' and then it asks me if there's anything else I want included in the next chapter, so I tell it to throw in some hot broads, lesbians maybe, and some pro sports action plus a big sword battle like they have in that sexy-violent-weird medieval show that plays on premium cable, just to spice things up.

CHAPTER II

With the potent smell of burning wood proliferating throughout their modest bungalow, the Fuerst family sat around a homemade kitchen table, eating their Christmas dinner in abject silence.

Both boys—Heinrich and Wolfgang—had fresh bruises upon their necks and backs, the result of having failed to have had their room in an acceptable state prior to its daily inspection earlier that morning. Their father had ignored their pleas for mercy, brutally pummeling each boy with his favorite tool of punishment—an old baseball bat he'd found behind a little league diamond shortly after arriving in the United States, most likely discarded by a spoiled child who'd received a newer version of the same toy from his parents.

The abject decadence and boundless wastefulness of Americans never ceased to amaze the former German peasant.

Since settling in rural Wisconsin a dozen years earlier, Reinhard had become a well-respected tradesman in the small town of Waterford. His formidable skills as a carpenter and constant volunteer work had made him a popular member of the tightly-knit, insular community. The charismatic Austrian immigrant easily won over all those he came in contact with by virtue of an uncanny ability to seem both charming and captivatingly harmless. Reinhard demonstrated at all times a carefree yet dignified demeanor which served him well during his integration into post-war American life.

When asked about his WWII experiences, Fuerst would effortlessly perform one of his well-rehearsed soliloquies demonizing the Nazis and Communists as the 'joint incarnations of pure evil'. Having been drafted into service late in the war, he had deserted the wretched Nazi war machine and had been in hiding when the armistice was signed, escaping to America and the 'blessed land of the free' soon after his Austrian village had been overrun by the vicious Red Army.

While deep down he was mortified by the words that he was forced to spew in keeping his true identity secret, Fuerst knew that Himmler would have understood, and even endorsed, his need to denounce National Socialism as a means of survival in their cause's new host nation.

As his fellow Nazis had stood trial at Nuremburg, reintegrated into post-war life, or escaped to South America with the aid of an elaborate network of sympathetic bureaucrats, Reinhard had made it to America purely through his own cunning and ingenuity. No one in the Reich had known of his plans to flee Bakum and travel across the Atlantic with his young family. By now there was nothing, no physical evidence at least, tracing him to the Order of the Black Sun, the SS, or Himmler. No one on Earth had any idea what had become of Reinhard Krauss during or after World War II, and he was presumed dead by both German and Allied authorities in the fall of 1948.

Reinhard's twin sons had by now matured into highly capable adolescent boys, each exhibiting dynamic abilities well beyond their thirteen years of life. Dr. Genzken's serum had given Heinrich exceptional intellectual ability and had molded

Wolfgang into an amazing physical specimen. Already nearing six feet in height, young Wolf was a local celebrity before he could shave, his athletic prowess rapidly becoming the stuff of legend throughout Racine County and southern Wisconsin. Meanwhile, as his brother was claiming track and field records at an unprecedented rate, Heinrich was earning academic accolades galore. His faculty for mathematics, languages, biology, and chemistry, for which he showed a particular affinity, all neared genius levels in only the sixth grade. His strict father forbade him from skipping ahead into high school however, preferring he remain with Wolfgang and other children his own age.

While their schoolmates were opening presents and attending church services on this particular Christmas Night, the Fuerst brothers readied for another evening of 'instruction' in the secret basement chamber Reinhard had built soon after purchasing their unassuming dwelling in the autumn of 1946.

The twins were by now very used to the daily exercises their father had crafted for their benefit, having attended this second, esoteric school every night since they had been in kindergarten. Reinhard had transformed their cellar into a near-exact replica of Wewelsburg's ceremonial hall, complete with grandiose imagery representing the multiple deities which the Order of the Black Sun had incorporated into their construction of Himmler's grand religious doctrine.

During Reinhard's time with the SS, a pair of Nazi mystics named Hellmuf Wolff and A. Frank Glahn had revealed to him an ancient Gypsy potion which infiltrated and greatly diluted the consciousness of those who took it, significantly negating their ability to resist the power of suggestion and ultimately allowing its server complete control over their helpless, submissive victim.

BRYCE ALLEN

Composed mainly of several barbiturates and Deuterocohnia leaves, the Wolff-Glahn Concoction had proved remarkably successful in several tests in which it had been utilized in the early 1940s, its immense potential never fully realized due to the Allied victory over the Axis. Using a diluted version of this mind control potion, Reinhard was able to command his sons' complete devotion and attention during his evening lectures, in which he educated the heirs to an as-yet-unclaimed ethereal empire in the ways of the occult, Nazism and the Black Sun. The Fuerst Family was destined for greatness. Of that there was no doubt.

In his spare time, the Fuersts' patriarch devoted his time to writing science fiction and fantasy, a curious affectation that even Reinhard himself did not completely understand. He had taken a liking to Jules Verne and J.R.R. Tolkien shortly after arriving in the U.S. and felt compelled to create fictional worlds of his own, as if possessed by some external, all-powerful calling... As his sons now studied *Mein Kampf*, Reinhard retired to his study to pound away on the secondhand typewriter he'd bought at a local swap meet he'd attended during the sultry summer of 1951[5].

The clandestine Nazi cracked his knuckles and got straight to work, pounding mercilessly upon the metallic keys that in turn hammered a series of words onto cheap paper, creating something magical that Fuerst was certain would one day be a best-seller and afford him the opportunity to make an indelible mark upon a culture he would ultimately control. Set in an alternate reality in which the supercontinent of Pangaea had never broken apart, Reinhard Fuerst's operatic text brimmed with drama, action, political intrigue—all the great hallmarks of classic literature... The

---

[5] Extraneous [ik-strey-nee-uh s], adjective.
  1. Introduced or coming from without; not belonging or proper to a thing; external; foreign: extraneous substances in our water.
  2. Not pertinent; irrelevant: an extraneous remark; extraneous decoration.

27

first volume of what would be a multi-book narrative chronicling several generations of the characters and universe he'd created centered upon a disgraced gladiator forced into military service at the behest of an unscrupulous Propaganda Minister[6] with a hidden agenda[7].

Set in the midst of a decades-old war in which the two superpowers of the mono-continental world (one to the north and one to the south) found themselves immersed in a constant mode of battle, the opening movement of the PANGAEAVERSE SAGA chronicled the attempt of the southern nation-state's military to mount the world's first-ever naval assault, journeying around the south pole across the mega ocean known as Panthalassa. Reinhard entitled his ambitious debut novel...

---

[6] Redundant [ri-duhn-duh nt], adjective.
1. Characterized by verbosity or unnecessary repetition in expressing ideas; prolix: a redundant style.
2. Being in excess; exceeding what is usual or natural: a redundant part.
3. Having some unusual or extra part or feature.
4. Characterized by superabundance or superfluity: lush, redundant vegetation.

[7] Repetitive [ri-pet-i-tiv], adjective.
Pertaining to or characterized by repetition.

WAVEFRONT

CHAPTER 1

It was a gloomy, blustery evening[8]. A single bolt of lightning dashed ominously across the horizon, the deafening boom of its accompanying thunder drowning out the volatile heckles being yelped out by the drunken rabble on hand at Astarte Stadium.

Badyn Taylor grasped the game ball resolutely in his right hand as a firmly-clenched left fist collided with an opposing euzon's jaw, a smattering of blood flashing across his filthy uniform just as the skies opened up and a heavy rain began to fall upon the playing field.

The Peltasts' star pincer glanced up at the game merk to see the seconds ticking away, the score deadlocked at ten apiece. He quickly scanned the field for any teammates in better position than he to attempt the winning

---

[8] From Wikipedia: The Bulwer-Lytton Fiction Contest (BLFC) is a tongue-in-cheek contest held annually and is sponsored by the English Department of San Jose State University in San Jose, California. Entrants are invited "to compose the opening sentence to the worst of all possible novels"—that is, deliberately bad. The contest was started in 1982 by Professor Scott E. Rice of the English Department at San Jose State University and is named for English novelist and playwright Edward George Bulwer-Lytton, author of the much-quoted first line "It was a dark and stormy night".

caedo. Finding only victims of an oppressive defensive scheme within eyesight, Taylor acted swiftly, taking three purposeful steps prior to heaving the discus-shaped projectile forward with all of his might.

A pair of gambits collided into New Tyre's captain just as he released the shot, several of his ribs cracking loudly as he collapsed into a heap of agony beneath his bulky assailants. With North Dion's two largest players smothering him, Bishop was unable to witness the spinning ball he'd launched breach its metallic target, the game merk loudly expiring a split second later to give the Peltasts a dramatic victory.

Astarte Stadium erupted into a riotous uproar as the summa radis signaled the successful score, the vanquished North Dion gambits cursing loudly as they liberated Bishop from his makeshift envelopment prior to hastily evacuating the playing area. Bishop struggled to his feet as his teammates rushed over to congratulate him, a boisterous public address announcer loudly proclaiming that a new WLPS record for most caedos in a single season had just been set by New Tyre's favorite son.

"Way to go, Badyn!" an excited rookie shouted as he embraced his captain amidst a calamitous celebration. Taylor winced as his freshly-broken ribs knifed into his innards at the young toxote's behest.

"Verp off, kid!" Taylor growled at the over-anxious youngster, shoving him to the ground as a harsh grimace engraved itself upon his rugged visage. His fellow Peltasts gave him some breathing room as the team doctor rushed over to the scene, brandishing a kit jam-packed with state-of-the-art medical supplies.

"You okay, Cap? That hit looked pretty bad." The doctor's eyes were wide with alarm as he struggled to catch his breath in the wake of a frantic thirty orgye dash.

Gathering his senses, Taylor managed to force away the intense pain affronting his midsection. "Just a couple of broken ribs. I'll survive." The valiant sportsman's words resounded with an overt stoicism, his capacious machismo absolute[9].

The remainder of New Tyre's roster stayed behind as Dr. Malta escorted their leader off of the field, the crowd eagerly showering professional streamball's new single-season caedo champion with brazen adulation. Before making his way into the locker room area, Taylor reluctantly raised his arm to salute the Peltasts faithful as he removed his mud-covered kranos. He broadcast an enigmatic smile that drew shrieks of approval from the female fans in attendance as he shook the hand of his patiently-waiting head coach.

"That was a hell of a toss, Badyn," Coach Adams offered, a hint of truculence infiltrating his tone[10]. He glared at his captain with a palpable disdain, a look the veteran pincer was all too familiar with.

"Just another day at the office." Taylor spat a globule of blood onto the moist terrain. "That win get us in the playoffs?"

"Yeah, unless Platea beats Byrsa later tonight. Can't see that happening though."

---

[9] From Wikipedia: In literary criticism, purple prose is prose text that is so extravagant, ornate, or flowery as to break the flow and draw excessive attention to itself. Purple prose is characterized by the extensive use of adjectives, adverbs, zombie nouns, and metaphors. When it is limited to certain passages, they may be termed purple patches or purple passages, standing out from the rest of the work.

[10] Annoying [uh-noi-ing], adjective.
1. causing annoyance; irritatingly bothersome
2. constantly having to check footnotes in a shitty novel

"Good. Tell the quaestors I want my bonus in thallars this time, not acros." Taylor coldly ignored several young fans' pleas for an autograph as he disappeared into a concrete-encased passageway reserved exclusively for team personnel.

Adams apologized to a suddenly-weeping toddler on his star player's behalf prior to following Taylor down into the shadow-riddled tunnel. "I'll see what I can do," Adams stated ruefully. "By the way, the commissioner wants to talk to you before you do your post-game press conference."

"What the kreit does that old bastard want?"

"I've got no idea. He probably just wants to bask in the glow of the Dominion's most famous athlete for a few minutes."

"Yeah, well he'd better not be planning on basking for too long. I've got a balnae to visit after all of this nonsense is over with."

Adams flung his arms up in disgust. "You're a class act, Badyn. A real class act." The middle-aged coach stopped walking and turned back towards the playing field, a look of extreme remorse upon his sullen face. Also, two super-hot lesbians were totally making out in the stands somewhere. Totally. A sword fight happened at some point as well. Yup.

《《———》》》

I wake up in a cold sweat and somehow my zPad's batteries are dead, so I grab an AirMall magazine and flip to the page advertising these special bras with water in them and go to the bathroom to jerk off.

《《《——》》》

The plane lands and I wait until everyone is off before I depart for the terminal. I grab my bags and head to the car rental zone. The clerk at the counter I approach has a weird complexion that I've never seen before. His skin is aggressive in its beigeness and awkwardly drapes a bulbous forehead and impossibly thin face in a greyish hue that seems almost extraterrestrial.

"Salve. Help you may I, amicus?" the alien-looking dude asks me. Of course his accent is all kinds of weird too—half Australian, half West African or something. His nametag says his name is 'Acacius Zipp'. Interesting handle.

"Um, yeah, I need a… car." I'm sure I'm radiating all kinds of discomfort, but the guy doesn't seem to notice. Or maybe he's just used to it and doesn't care. Good for him then if that's the case.

"Bonum, cars we have copia." Acacius cracks his knuckles and starts hammering on the keyboard of his computer in an exaggerated, animated typing style that might be funny to some people—Eskimos, for example.

"Peregrinatione well hodie, sir?" Acacius asks me.

I'm not sure what the hell language this guy is mixing his English with, so I just nod and ask him where he's from. He tells me he's Rodinian and asks me, I think, what kind of car I want.

"Just a midsize is good. I don't care what make." I take out my trusty credit card and hand it to the guy and he runs it through, seemingly unable to make eye contact with me. Acacius has me sign some papers for insurance and such and then hands me the keys to a domestic sedan.

"Thank you," I say, folding the paperwork under my arm. The alien clerk smiles and nods at me as I walk away from his counter, totally forgetting to ask him about his country's deposed

33

king or if the rebel army's butchered any of his relatives as of yet. Ah well. Next time.

<<<—>>>

I check into a motel somewhere in the San Fernando Valley and flirt with the Ms. Trailer Park USA pageant-reject of a concierge for a while until she mentions that she's got a fiancé. I call her a 'cock tease' which is an overreaction I suppose but there's not much I can do about it after it's left my mouth and all, is there?

My room's a lot cleaner than I was expecting which is a nice surprise. I call the office of that Hollywood dude who emailed me about Iris on the motel landline and a voice recording tells me they're closed until the morning, which makes sense since it's pretty late and all[11].

There's nothing good on TV and I promised myself I wouldn't hit up any strip clubs on this trip, so I decide to just buy a six-pack of suds from a nearby gas station and fire my zPad back up so as to continue reading the exploits of the Fuerst Family and that crazy Nazi-writer dad guy. Good times.

---

[11] From Wikipedia: A time zone is a region that observes a uniform standard time for legal, commercial, and social purposes. Time zones tend to follow the boundaries of countries and their subdivisions because it is convenient for areas in close commercial or other communication to keep the same time.

CHAPTER III

The patrons at Freddy's Book Emporium looked on with modest disinterest as Reinhard Fuerst, AKA Reginald Tilden[12], took a seat and began to read from his recently-released debut novel, WAVEFRONT. Heinrich and Wolfgang Fuerst sat attentively at the back of the room amidst the dozen-odd ostensible literary enthusiasts who'd elected to spend their Sunday afternoon listening to an unknown sci-fi/fantasy author recite some prose.

"Thank you for coming today," Reinhard said as the clock on the wall nearest to him struck 2:00 p.m. exactly. "I'll be reading an excerpt from my new book this afternoon, I hope you like it."

The Nazi war criminal cleared his throat and opened the freshly-pressed hardcover edition of WAVEFRONT to a page early on in the proceedings...

---

[12] From Wikipedia: A pen name, nom de plume (/ˌnɒm də ˈpluːm/, French: [nõ də plym]), or literary double is a pseudonym adopted by an author. A pen name may be used to make the author's name more distinctive, to disguise his or her gender, to distance an author from some or all of his or her previous works, to protect the author from retribution for his or her writings, to combine more than one author into a single author, or for any of a number of reasons related to the marketing or aesthetic presentation of the work. The author's name may be known only to the publisher or may come to be common knowledge.

WAVEFRONT

CHAPTER 2

Badyn Taylor enjoyed a euphoric three seconds of silence before Viennet Duca, the Peltasts' jittery Propaganda Officer, rushed to his side. "Commissioner Segal just wants five minutes in private with you before you talk to the media. He's waiting for you in the Bacchhus Dry Lounge." The dwarfish adjutant offered the sweat-blood-and-mud-soaked streamballer a bottle of ElectoSucus. New Tyre's M.V.P. greedily snatched the green plastic jug from Duca's hand, devouring its non-carbonated contents in a single swig.

Taylor released a loud groan of approval upon guzzling back the rehydrating fluid, his constitution miraculously restored. "Yeah, sure thing, Duke, I'll be there in a second. I should probably clean myself up if I'm going to meet with the commish."

"Okay, no problem, I'll let Segal know." Duca sauntered down the corridor, barking for the clamoring, writhing mob of journalists to be patient and to stay behind the crimson partition that had been erected earlier that week in anticipation of Acacius Muldoon's hallowed caedo record being broken.

Taylor sighed animatedly as he retreated into a small, players-only lavatory at the end of the hallway, immediately locking the old-fashioned door behind him. He ran some cold water from a filthy faucet and splashed it upon the rounded peak of his shorn skull prior to reluctantly gazing into a grime-caked mirror, into a pair of lifeless eyes peering out from behind the ironclad face of a seasoned gladiator.

• • • • •

Constane Segal was beginning to grow impatient.

Leaning against a marble pillar in a dark, empty lounge, the first-year commissioner caught himself grinding his teeth, a bad habit he'd picked up back in his army days that had stayed with him throughout his decades in government and now, apparently, into his new post as leader of the World League of Professional Streamball.

The commissioner had arrived in New Tyre the previous evening and had spent his time in the provincial capital largely in seclusion, not wanting the media to get wind of his presence. Since assuming the role of WLPS Commissioner, Segal had kept a relatively low profile, preferring to let his underlings take turns in the spotlight in favor of focusing on effectively running an increasingly-profitable sporting enterprise.

Badyn Taylor's march towards history had increased the league's popularity tremendously during Segal's first season in command. Attendance, digitron ratings, and merchandise sales had all gone up dramatically, citizens throughout the Dominion having followed Taylor's ever-climbing caedo total with feverous interest.

But now it was over. The record had been broken. A hype-fueled journey had reached its logical conclusion, just as everyone involved had hoped for and expected. It was all somewhat anticlimactic, truth be told.

Faced in a similar situation, a lesser commissioner might simply publicly congratulate Taylor and canonize him in the press, get as much mileage out of the momentous achievement as possible. But not Constane Segal. No, for him the record was only the beginning of something much bigger, something more substantial—something innovative and ground-breaking... Something truly great.

The next chapter in the history of Segal's WLPS would begin here, in an empty room which, at the moment, resonated with a brooding silence that seemed almost supernatural.

Segal pulled back upon his tunic sleeve to check his wristmerk yet again, his frustration mounting. While he was indeed grateful to Taylor for having played a pivotal role in his master plan to strengthen the WLPS' position as the Dominion's most powerful professional sports league and one of its best-run corporations, Segal was in no mood to waste any more time in the depths of a lackluster stadium waiting for a dimwitted streamballer to reveal himself.

At long last the room's main entrance flickered in a brilliant cavalcade of neon light particles as the mountainous frame of Badyn Taylor passed through the imitation-oak-framed holographic barrier.

"You wanted to see me?" Taylor asked, his deep, masculine voice belied by the naïve-sounding cadence of a schoolchild.

"Sit down Badyn, please." Segal motioned towards an empty steel fauteuil chair which sat at an odd angle in front of a baize-top table situated at the center of the room. Taylor hesitated for a moment before acquiescing to his boss' request.

The cold, metallic chair was able to accommodate Taylor's large body with no small amount of difficulty. "It's weird seeing this place empty," Taylor playfully declared as he forced himself into the smallish chair. "Usually it's jammed with rowdy season ticket holders and sponsors, y'know?"

Segal allowed a wry grin to creep across his stern, weathered face. "Yes, well I made special arrangements for us to meet in private."

The elderly statesman lurched forward as he awkwardly made his way over to the edge of the table at which sat the Dominion's most celebrated sportsman. He folded his arms behind his back as he walked, just as an aristocrat from another century might've done during a leisurely afternoon stroll.

Once he reached his destination he made sure to stand in close enough proximity to Taylor to make him as uncomfortable as possible. It was a trick he'd learned during his tenure as ambassador to Genserica. Staring menacingly down into his guest's wide-set eyes, he purposefully allowed the ominous disquiet that bounded throughout the room adequate time to seep into Taylor's veins.

"Congratulations are in order I'd say," Segal stated after a moment, continuing to dominate his subject in a covertly-alpha manner. "That game-winning caedo was your sixty-second of the season, yes? A new league record... Very impressive, very impressive indeed." Judging by the blank expression on Taylor's face, Segal could tell that the sardonic tone he'd skillfully made use of had been wasted completely on the dimwitted ignoramus currently in his company.

"My teammates deserve a lot of the credit for my success," Taylor instinctively replied, commencing a contrived spiel which had likely been spoon-fed to him by Peltasts management. "Coach Adams really took a chance switching me from gambit to pincer as well, but the real reason I'm doing so well is the New Tyre fans, they really give me a boost every time I—"

"Cut the cern, Badyn," Segal interrupted, assertively. "Let me see it."

"Let you see what?" Taylor replied, feigning offense.

Grinning diabolically to reveal a yellowish set of ragged teeth, Segal began the speech he'd been preparing in his mind since his arrival in New Tyre the previous night. "I know you were contacted by a man named Blandus Anders back in Peret," he said, accusingly. "I know he offered to... enhance your physical abilities through less than reputable means. My sources tell me that you underwent the procedure during the first week of Tebetu, while you were allegedly on vacation with your wife in East Baltica. Do you dispute that these events took place, Badyn?"

Taylor's grey eyes bulged wide, an expression of disbelief washing over his face. His mouth swung open as he struggled to speak, stumbling over his words as if running an obstacle course whilst high on cesariana. "I... listen here, Commissioner... there..."

"Save the excuses—I'm not interested," Segal snapped. "Now. Let me see it."

Taylor lowered his bald, bulbous head in shame. He slowly raised his right arm and reached across his body with his left. He pulled back on his sleeve to reveal an impeccably-sculpted bicep, a small scar engraved upon its summit. After taking a deep, expressive breath, Taylor dug into the scar with a calloused index finger. He pulled down upon what appeared to be some kind of rubbery, synthetic flesh panel to reveal a rectangular-shaped circuit board embedded within the dense muscular fabric surrounding his thick humerus.

The commissioner leaned forward to inspect the robotic appendage closely, his badly-wrinkled face collapsing into a labyrinth of unsightly creases as his steel green eyes narrowed into an intense, deliberate squint.

"Impressive craftsmanship." Segal stood up straight and put his hand on Taylor's shoulder. "Now, shall we discuss the manner in which we will deal with this brazen act of perfidiousness?"

Badyn Taylor nodded solemnly, the bitter, unfamiliar taste of defeat pillaging his palette.

《《《——》》》

An old-fashioned touchtone phone stationed on the nightstand next to my bed starts wailing and I fall out of bed trying to grab the receiver. I finally get a hold of the thing and that same, allegedly-engaged slut from yesterday tells me that she's making my wakeup call. Bitch.

The water pressure in the shower here sucks and, apparently, I left my toiletry bag back in Europe, so my day isn't off to a great start. I make my way back down to the lobby and scarf down some shitty eggs and toast as part of my complimentary continental breakfast. There's an older guy eating at a table close to mine and he's got a metal leg, so I ask him how he lost his organic one. He turns around and tells me, flatly, to mind my own business so I do.

《《《——》》》

It takes me about 45 minutes to find showbiz player extraordinaire Robert Anderson's office, which is on the ground floor of this rundown mini-mall in a shady-looking neighborhood north of Sherman Oaks. I spill my coffee as I get out of my rental car and swear in a language I didn't realize I knew. A hot young mom pushing a stroller through the parking lot tells me to watch my language around her children and I tell her to fuck off. In English. I think.

《《《——》》》

Anderson Talent Brokers, Inc. doesn't have anyone manning the front desk when I walk in. There's one of those little bell thingies sitting there though so I ring that a few times until this nerdy-looking dude in a cheap suit appears.

"May I help you sir?" the dork asks me.

"You Anderson?"

"Who's asking?"

"Shane Bishop."

"Oh, you're Iris' father," the dink sighs, wiping his sweaty brow. "I thought you were a process server or something."

I take my sunglasses off and do a bad impression of a TV cop as I ask him why he would think that. "Going through a divorce or have some unpaid bills, Captain Big Shot?"

"Just a misunderstanding with a former client," he says, anxiously. "Happens all the time out here."

"La La Land, right?"

"That's right..." He shuffles towards me and offers his hand, which I shake in the customary fashion with which I'm sure you are familiar. "Please, step into my office, Mr. Bishop."

Anderson motions for me to follow him so I do. "Call me Shane," I say, instructingly[13]. The corridor leading to his office is dirty and poorly lit. This entire operation reeks of amateurishness[14]. I wish I could say I was surprised that Iris was in league with this clown, but the fact of the matter is she was never that bright so... yeah.

"When did you get into town?" Anderson asks as we reach his office, which consists solely of a department store desk and some cheap wooden chairs. A few certificates/diplomas adorn the walls along with pictures of this asshole hanging out with Z-level celebs at shitty-looking parties. Like I said: Grade A Dink.

"Last night." I sit down. He does the same.

"Long way to travel. You're based out of eastern Europe now, correct?"

---

[13] Nope, not a word.

[14] This one's a real word. What a language!

"Something like that, yeah."

"I see…" Anderson's getting nervous. He probably doesn't deal with many guys like me in his line of work. I decide to amp up the roguishness. Just for kicks. And to speed things up.

"Daughter. Missing. What's the story, Agent Boy?"

Anderson sighs yet again and goes out of his way to avoid looking me in the eye. Pussy. He tells me that he took Iris on as a client a few months ago, even though she didn't have any experience in the entertainment industry whatsoever.

"What do you charge the wannabes that stumble in here?" I try to remember exactly how much money I gave Iris in the middle section of the last book we were in together and then try to sort out exactly what this agent's 'motivation' is but then I force said thoughts out of my brain once Anderson answers.

"Nothing crazy… A few hundred at first then we take a slice of whatever gigs we can get them."

"No shortage of delusional losers in this part of the country, huh Mister Anderson?"

"Look man, it's a living okay? What line of work are you in exactly, Shane?"

"Bible sales. When did my daughter disappear?"

"Last week. I talked to her on her way to an acting class in Santa Monica, told her about an audition the next morning I'd booked for her. She never made it."

"To the class?"

"No, the audition."

"What was the role?"

"Small part in a horror flick."

"When did you file the report with the cops?

"A couple of days after that… Her cell stopped working and I swung by her apartment, but no one was there."

"Thanks for your concern. Did she have any friends out here? Aside from yourself obviously."

"Not that I'm aware of... She had you down on her client form as her next of kin but only had that email address listed for contact info."

"We're not exactly 'close.'"

"None of my business, Mister... Shane. I just know you used to be a cop or a P.I. or something to that effect and that you might be able to track Iris down before the L.A.P.D. can."

"If she's still alive that is." Anderson is taken aback by the casual manner in which I deliver this line. He tries to make some crack about me having a 'particular set of skills' that will help me find my daughter which I guess is supposed to be a reference to some movie or TV show but whatever it is I haven't seen it, so I just glower back at the guy until he stops giggling nervously and pretends to clear his throat.

"What's the deal with the acting class that Iris went to in Santa Monica?" I ask. "Is it a regular thing or was it a one-off?"

"It's a regular class. They're meeting tonight actually, here's the address." Anderson scribbles down the info on a loose piece of paper he grabs from an open drawer. He slides it over to me slowly, his expression completely blank. I snatch the thing greedily and shove it in my pocket.

"Thanks," I say, staring the agent down. It seems like he wants to tell me something else, so I wait for that but then he doesn't say shit and I just get up and leave.

«‹‹—››»

I have a few hours to kill before the class starts so I go to a bar and throw back a few cold ones. No one really wants to chat and the pool table's out of order, so I bust out my magic zPad and open the LiveStory app to do some more reading. Apparently now that Reinhard guy's sons are grown up and he's a successful writer with a fringe cult thing starting to develop on the side. Good for him. Not sure I like that though, so I stop reading Chapter IV, go back to the main screen part of the program and tell it to kill Reinhard off, pronto. Boo yah. It takes a minute or so for the program to respond and then it asks me if I'd like any other changes and I tell it to make the story more like that movie from the '90s where the retard from Alabama experiences history and junk because that was badass.

CHAPTER V

Ludington High's graduating class had two prominent students absent from what was the largest convocation in the institution's history, its first wave of Baby Boomers rolling off of the educational assembly line into 'adulthood'–long before the term was a mere semantic abstraction. It seemed that the school's Class Valedictorian and Male Athlete of the Year both had more pressing matters to attend to on this particular day, the warmest on record in Racine County history.

As the oft-mocked school principal Richard Steenis had called their names in absentia, Heinrich and Wolfgang Fuerst were several miles away, standing over their father's foreboding, freshly-sealed grave. The twins found themselves choking back tears as, for the first time in their young lives, they suddenly felt no sense of firm, immediate direction.

This was a far more frightening prospect than Reinhard's baseball bat had ever been.

It had all been so sudden–the heart attack, the hospital, the ritual, the funeral arrangements… As the stark reality of their situation was finally beginning to sink in, the Fuerst brothers were suddenly confronted with a very different brand of fear than the bombastic trepidation their father had instilled in them the past eighteen years.

While neither boy had particularly fond memories of their domineering, violent father, they nonetheless knew that the oath he had sworn to Heinrich Himmler two decades earlier was now theirs to fulfill, a lifetime of strict instruction having supposedly paved the way for their path to immense glory. The pseudo-religious group Reinhard had formed in the wake of his book series' success had been quickly disbanded following his untimely demise. A few members had even gone so far as to commit suicide out of grief at the sudden loss of their new leader. Local police had investigated the circumstances surrounding the deaths but both Wolfgang and Heinrich were able to plead ignorance as they'd known little of their father's dealings with the group. A dimwitted detective had stumbled upon the Spear of Destiny whilst investigating the Church's modest headquarters and temporarily held it in an evidence room before Heinrich had managed to convince him that it was a harmless family heirloom and of incredible senti-mental value to the grieving orphan. The detective had handed it back over to the teenager with a shrug, wholly unaware of the dire consequences of this seemingly innocuous action…

On his deathbed, the Fuerst Family patriarch had revealed to his sons the effectual mind control technique he himself had been taught during his time with the Order of the Black Sun. The recipe for the Wolff-Glahn Concoction had passed through Reinhard's lips along with his final breaths. Heinrich instantly stored the formula within the massive confines of his brilliant mind, already thinking of ways to both use it and enhance its effectiveness.

The most dangerous brainwashing potion in human history, a tool of sublime power, was now in the possession of two teenagers from Wisconsin by way of Nazi Germany. Both boys accepted their weighty inheritance without reservation.

Having by now matured into highly-capable young men with truly incredible abilities, the Fuersts were the most talked-about siblings in all of Wisconsin. Tales of their exploits and accomplishments echoed from county to county as the 'Genius and the Giant' became unlikely, reluctant folk heroes throughout the Badger State.

With his perfect S.A.T. score, exemplary grade-point-average, and off-the-charts I.Q. in tow, Heinrich had received dozens of scholarship offers from Ivy League schools throughout the United States. Wolfgang too had received multiple scholarship offers—from universities anxious for him to lead their Division I football programs to a national title as either a linebacker or tailback, both positions he had an unequivocal mastery of as evidenced by his 15 tackle, six touchdown performance in the legendary Wisconsin High School State Championship Game of '63.

Much to the consternation of their recruitment agents, guidance counselors, peers, coaches, and teachers alike however, neither boy seemed the least bit interested in post-secondary education however.

Instead, throughout their final year at Ludington, they had planned to travel abroad after graduation, ostensibly to 'discover their roots' but in reality to train with the offspring of other former Nazis at a secret institution known as the Academy of National Socialist Advancement.

In what had ultimately been the final year of his life, Reinhard Fuerst/Krauss had reestablished contact with other former SS members with calculated reticence and care, learning of the arcane training center for aspiring neo-Nazis during his boys' junior year of high school while also tending to his duties as a Cult Leader and novelist. It had been his wish that Heinrich and Wolfgang attend The Academy in the fall of '63. His sudden death put the plan in limbo however, leaving his twin sons with a curious crisis of conscience with which to deal.

The ever-rebellious Heinrich had absolutely no intention of leaving the U.S. He had silently questioned his increasingly-deranged father's rationale for contacting his former compatriots and did not see the need to abandon the country he one day planned to rule. Who were these European neo-Nazis, after all, but a collection of failed soldiers—has-beens and never-weres? He deemed them all to be completely out of touch with modernity and the paradigm shift in global politics that had made their archaic form of totalitarianism obsolete. Heinrich had by now crafted his own, unique form of absolute government—a kind of laissez-faire autocracy that would one day be either embraced by or imposed upon the masses, leaving democracy, communism and fascism all by the wayside.

Heinrich was intent upon traveling across America in the coming months, living a romanticized bohemian existence in cities and towns of various sizes so as to gauge the will of ordinary citizens. He planned to incorporate their primal fears and desires into a grand political ideology that would one day reign supreme in the annals of world history.

Wolfgang, meanwhile—ever more cautious and reserved than his fraternal twin—was reluctant to disobey Reinhard's dying order. The sense of freedom he felt was far more frightening than liberating as the iron will of his father was all Wolfgang had ever known to follow. When his brother channeled their father's visceral anger in demanding he stay in America however, the hulking football star was quick to acquiesce. He agreed to burn their plane tickets to Europe along with a myriad of other documents Reinhard had drawn up over the years—blueprints for a new Order of the Black Sun that Wolfgang and Heinrich had by now memorized. Elements of the Order's modus operandi had begun to surface in Reinhard's embryonic Church in the final months of his life, but only the very tip of a sinister iceberg had been revealed to the nascent religion's followers.

A growing rift between the Fuerst brothers had expanded exponentially in recent weeks, with Reinhard's decision to have Wolfgang, and Wolfgang only, perform the Order of the Black Sun's death ritual upon him in his final hours having infuriated Heinrich greatly. Heinrich now saw his brother as little more than a dim-witted nuisance he needed to rid himself of as soon as possible. *The oaf is holding you back… You must fulfill the oath on your own—prove your worth, lay claim to the greatness Father foretold of…*

Now seated next to one another at a near-empty train station, a densely-packed canvas bag slung formally over each of their shoulders, the Fuerst brothers ultimately resolved to go their separate ways. They were, for the time being at least, set to explore the world on their own terms while retaining the sense of duty bestowed upon them by the last of the Knights of the Order of the Black Sun. The brothers vowed to meet again when the time was right to fulfill their destiny and lay claim to the awesome power that was their birthright.

Following a quick coin toss, it was determined that Heinrich would board a train heading east while Wolfgang would journey west, both men suddenly alone for the first time in their lives. They each found the sense of solitude which soon engulfed them strangely exhilarating.

《《《——》》》

I wander around a random mall for a while and then I get hungry, so I eat a slice of pizza and a huge bowl of frozen yogurt for dessert. Yummy.

Some asshole dressed up like Dracula decides to start randomly killing shoppers with an assault rifle on the floor beneath me so I watch that for a while and then I grab a pizza slicer from the same joint I just dined at and slide down a concrete support column to where the shooter's at and I sneak up behind the guy and slit his throat, pressing my thumb down hard against the razor-sharp wheel thingy to keep it from rotating as the prick gurgles something about Jesus loving me as he dies. I take an escalator back up to the food court and help myself to some free frozen yogurt since all the employees are gone or hiding and then I head back out to the parking lot and drive away just as the cops are finally arriving.

《《《——》》》

The rec center that hosts the weekly acting class Iris went to before she disappeared is pretty shoddy and I guess I'm a little early since there's a bunch of kids workshopping some play there when I walk through the door. An older guy who I guess must be the director turns around and shoots me a *what the fuck?!?* look when I enter the joint and then he holds a finger up to his lips, which is dummy sign language for 'shut the hell up, asshole'[15].

I stand totally still at the back of this big open room and the kids on stage keep doing their dramatic theater nonsense. This decent-looking broad in blue yoga pants hugs an ugly dude with bad skin and semi-yells: "This isn't just a halfway house anymore, Billy... It's a halfway *home!*"

Apparently, this is how the play ends because the older-director guy starts applauding vigorously after that bullshit line and the half-dozen fuckwads on the stage seem to relax a bit. I go to light a cigarette but then I remember I don't smoke.

"Bravo, bravo, bravo!" Director Man exclaims as he continues to clap like one of those cheap toy monkey wind-up things on about a pound-and-a-half of coke. He flicks his fancy-looking scarf up over his shoulder and prances up to the stage.

"You guys are really firing on all cylinders this week," the fairy says to the actors. "We are gonna *rock* this premiere on Friday night!"

The cast members start patting one another on the back and hugging each other and whatnot. All of them have this insane

---

[15] From Wikipedia: Nonverbal communication between people is communication through sending and receiving wordless cues. It includes the use of visual cues such as body language (kinesics), distance (proxemics) and physical environments/appearance, of voice (paralanguage) and of touch (haptics). It can also include chronemics (the use of time) and oculesics (eye contact and the actions of looking while talking and listening, frequency of glances, patterns of fixation, pupil dilation, and blink rate).

look of unabashed zeal in their young eyes and it's almost sickening, the enthusiasm they have for life at the moment. They'll learn. They'll learn.

After thoroughly taking care of stroking his actors' egos, the hammy theater veteran turns his attention back towards me. "Can I help you, sir?" he asks, really emphasizing a lisp that's downright serpentine.

"I'm looking for Iris Bishop."

"Yes, she's a student of mine, is she in some kind of trouble?" The queer affects an air of concern, briefly holding the hand attached to his limp wrist up to his mouth, as he makes his way over to the wall I'm leaning against. "I'm Stephen by the way, nice to meet you..." He extends the aforementioned appendage affixed to his aforementioned limp wrist and I shake it, gently.

"Shane. Shane Bishop. Iris is my daughter. She gets her looks from her mother. Obviously."

"Well, she should be here shortly—our evening class begins in a few minutes."

"Don't think so, pal. She's been officially designated a Missing Person by the state of California. The last time anyone heard from her was when she was on her way here for *your* class, Steve."

"Stephen... I'm sorry to hear she's gone missing—she's a promising student." The director again feigns a modicum of distress as he checks his watch, nervously.

"So, she was here last week then? For this class?" I ask, doing my best impression of a hardboiled detective from some 1930s dime novel, which we've previously established I'm quite good at[16]. The director nods. "Yes, yes she was."

---

[16] Allen, Bryce, The Spartak Trigger; ASIN: B00J27G8PI; Bedlam Press (An Imprint of Necro Publications), 2014

I ask him if he knows where she went after class let out and he starts to sweat, every ounce of cool he's got abandoning him in an instant. He shakes his head 'no' but it's pretty fucking obvious that he's lying.

"You sure?" I ask, aggressively. He shakes his head again, so I look around to make sure no one is looking—the shitty play's cast has by now dispersed—and I grab Stevie Boy by the throat and punch him in the stomach as hard as I can.

It takes a while for the fruit to catch his breath after he collapses in a heap of theatricality onto the rec center's cheap hardwood floor and curses me out for a while. I tell him I know he's lying and to tell me what he knows about Iris' disappearance ASAP or else I'll beat him to within a millimeter of his life. He shoots me a confused look, so I briefly explain the metric system to him[17]. After that's settled, the director starts weeping gently and tells me that it wasn't his fault.

"What wasn't your fault?" I start to motion like I might punch him again, but he winces, holds his hands up in a defensive manner and starts shouting "Okay, okay, okay!" before my fist's even clenched. I help Stephen get to his feet and he's panting heavily, his ruddy face flush with emotion.

"I'm not asking again, Steve."

The director whimpers and tells me that he'd agreed to let the Church of Solarism recruit new members at his acting classes in exchange for using their Hollywood connections to get him some bullshit role in a Blake Wilson movie. I ask him if Iris signed up for that junk and he nods his head and says he thinks so.

---

[17] From Wikipedia: The metric system is an internationally agreed decimal system of measurement. It was originally based on the mètre des Archives and the kilogramme des Archives introduced by the First French Republic in 1799 but over the years, the definitions of the metre and the kilogram have been refined, and the metric system has been extended to incorporate many more units.

"Great, so you got my daughter hooked up with some weirdo cult and now she's missing." I notice I'm grinding my teeth pretty badly and that's clearly making the director anxious because his body language is all 'don't hit me again' and whatnot and I think about maybe giving him a quick haymaker for shits and giggles but then some more wannabe movie stars show up for his next class, so I tell him to hope he doesn't see me again and I exit – stage left.

«««—»»»

The Church of Solarism's corporate/spiritual headquarters— the 'Silver Station'—is all the way out in Riverdale and it's closed by the time I get there so I make a mental note of what time they open in the morning—8:00am—and head back to my motel. For some reason every channel on TV is showing this old silent movie with dudes wearing white hoods fighting other dudes in blackface makeup and it's not very entertaining so I decide to do some more reading. I remind LiveStory about the retard-from-Alabama shit I want included in the book and then I crack open a beer and start flicking through some virtual pages. I get halfway through a chapter about the smart brother hanging out with a bunch of beatniks and a drugged-out movie star in New York and then he helps some artist with a silver wig kill the movie star right before some painting the guy made of her comes out so that his exhibition gets more publicity, but I hate the artsy fartsy direction things start to take so I flip back to the main screen and tell the program to make with some graphic violence already. It retcon-deletes all of the stupid/pretentious/lame New York junk and then starts Chapter VI over again…

56

CHAPTER VI

Crouching behind a pair of bullet-riddled corpses, Heinrich Fuerst held a grenade firmly in his right hand, waiting patiently for the deafening roar of machine gun fire to cease before acting.

His platoon had been ambushed five minutes earlier and, as far as he could tell, he was the sole survivor of a surprise Vietcong attack. As the advancing enemy soldiers yelped unintelligible phrases in their coarse native tongue, Fuerst hurriedly searched his fallen comrades' charred bodies for another weapon, his M-16 rifle having been lost in the initial mayhem of Charlie's brutal onslaught.

The young soldier was able to find a small pistol in the lapel pocket of his dead sergeant's third pattern jungle jacket, his heart hammering as the footsteps grew nearer and the gunfire became more sporadic. With the smell of still-burning flesh thick in the air, Fuerst pulled the pin on his grenade and lobbed it forward, momentarily channeling his brother's immense strength as the device flew almost fifty yards before landing and exploding – creating a perfect mix of destruction and distraction.

Heinrich had already taken out three VC soldiers by the time the grenade had gone off, darting in a zigzag pattern and firing his pistol with expert marksmanship—every bullet square through the heart of his target. As he suddenly heard the heart-dropping sounds of an empty chamber—*click, click, click*—Heinrich tossed his sidearm aside and leapt behind a nearby tree just as a half-dozen Vietcong soldiers finally spotted him and began firing their Chinese-made AK-47 assault rifles in his direction.

With the base of the tree behind which he knelt being torn apart by bullets, a crouching Fuerst drew a bowie knife from his right Bata boot and felt a phenomenal, almost supernatural calm overcome him. Soon the gunfire had stopped, and a thin metallic barrel was peeking through the splintered wood directly above Fuerst's head. Without hesitation, he grabbed the arms which held the weapon and flung them forward, the malnourished body of a frightened VC foot soldier—no older than sixteen—following. Fuerst plunged his bowie knife into the boy's chest, the resultant shriek prompting another round of enemy gunfire to erupt nearby.

Seizing the slain teenager's AK-47, Heinrich swiftly sprinted forward, several bullets whizzing past his head and shoulders as he leapt into a ditch that looked as if it had been dug by French soldiers during the early days of the war.

Turning quickly, Fuerst fired his weapon at the quintet of VC troops charging towards his makeshift bunker. Within seconds, all five were lying face down on the jungle floor and an eerie silence had overtaken the smoke-filled battleground.

Taking a deep breath, Fuerst felt a sharp pain in his left thigh and looked down to see an alarming amount of blood suddenly staining his tropical combat trousers. The second-generation Nazi quickly tore off one of his sleeves and used a half-hitch overhand knot to snugly tie the fabric around his upper leg, sufficiently stopping the bleeding.

As he limped forward, confident that no further threat existed, Fuerst heard a man meekly whimpering what sounded like common last words in the jungle– "Help... help me..."

Staggering over to a pile of bodies where the initial blast of the attack had struck, Fuerst found a member of his platoon–Private Howard Goldstein–badly burnt but still breathing, albeit with tremendous difficulty.

"Hank... thank God... you gotta get me outta here man..." the wounded soldier gasped through a still-noticeable New York accent.

Briefly looking around to make sure there were no other survivors, Heinrich pulled the clip out of his machine gun. He then took the one remaining bullet out of the chamber and knelt down next to the heavily-panting private, who was beset by a pair of extremely dead cousins from Alabama.

"What... what the hell... are you doing... Hank?? We gotta... go... now... help me up buddy, come on," Goldstein begged.

Having dropped his bowie knife at some point during the preceding firefight, Fuerst removed an M7 bayonet from the slowly-dying college dropout's rifle. He struck his final bullet twice–quickly and with great force, creating a cross-like imprint in the tip of the copper-jacketed projectile.

Fuerst then carefully placed the dum-dum back in the AK-47, loading the Soviet-designed gun in a single, fluid motion.

"Hank..." Goldstein pleaded, his breathing becoming more and more irregular as he clung desperately to life.

"Auf Wiedersehen, Juden," Fuerst said, aiming his weapon at the confused, panicked soldier's temple.

Goodbye, Jew.

Heinrich Fuerst, or Hank Dillon as he was known to the U.S. Army, pulled the trigger and bits of his platoon-mate's skull flew up and landed on his uniform as he felt a godlike power swelling through him. After taking sufficient time to appreciate the moment, he began marching south towards the Phu Bai Air Strip.

With a wounded leg the trek would take him several hours, but Reinhard Fuerst's eldest son was unworried with anything at the moment. A sense of unabashed invincibility had overtaken his demeanor as he limped forward, replaying the events of the previous twenty minutes over and over again in his mind's eye as a wry grin was cast upon his face. Fuerst/Dillon began to hum the opening stanzas of Wagner's *Parsifal* as he shuffled through the dense jungle terrain.

《《——》》》

I take a break from reading to take a piss and I can hear the people in the room next to mine having sex, so I imagine that the broad that's getting pounded looks something like that trashy/slutty-hot chick from the front desk and jerk off into the sink to the animal-like mating sounds they're making. I'm still not tired afterwards so I continue reading...

CHAPTER VII

His arms raised in triumph, Wolfgang Fuerst stood exultantly above his vanquished opponent as thousands of spectators cheered raucously and counted along with the referee.

"...seven... eight... nine... ten!!" the arena bellowed, formally concluding what had been a dramatically lopsided bout.

A brash, cocksure Austrian-American was now Heavyweight Boxing Champion of the World. He had won an event which promoters had dubbed 'The Melee on the Causeway' in a performance which would forever be remembered as 'The Boston Massacre' thanks to a clever article scribed by a journeyman sportswriter which was to soon find its way into national syndication.

This historic victory had been nearly eight years in the making.

Having moved to Nevada shortly after graduating from high school and turning down offers to play football from several high-profile collegiate programs, Wolfgang had taken a job as a janitor at a small boxing gymnasium in Reno. It wasn't long, however, before the towering teenager with a near-Herculean physique was being taught how to jab and then how to administer lethal punching combinations by a well-known, semi-retired trainer named Mitch 'Mad Dog' McKenna.

Within six months, Wolfgang was competing in amateur bouts throughout the Silver State, annihilating the competition with tremendous ease while McKenna continued to teach him the nuances of the sport. Fuerst proved to be a fast learner, and Mad Dog was incredibly excited to be training the most impressive physical specimen he'd encountered in nearly five decades in boxing. The experimental serum Wolfgang had been injected with as an infant had continued to evolve along with its host; both were now nearing their pinnacle in terms of strength and potency.

It had been nothing short of remarkable when, at the 1964 Olympic qualifiers in Colorado, a 19-year old kid from Wisconsin who had been fighting competitively for less than a year demolished every opponent he faced, resultantly earning the right to represent the United States at the Olympic Games in Japan.

Eventually winning the Gold Medal following a series of incredibly one-sided victories in the Heavyweight Division, Fuerst was an instant media darling—a good looking, articulate sportsman whose rise to the top had seemingly come out of nowhere.

Soon after his triumph in Tokyo, Fuerst entered the professional ranks, amassing a record of 12-0 before suffering a career-threatening shoulder injury in 1968, just as he was readying for his first title shot.

After taking a year off from boxing, 'Furious' Fuerst re-entered the ring to great fanfare with two of the most famous fights in the history of the sport pitting Wolf versus the reigning Heavyweight champion—an aging 'Brickyard' Bobby Williams. Both fights took place in Africa, and both ended in draws.

The first bout, the 'Boom Boom in Cameroon', was staged in an outdoor stadium and packed with nearly one hundred thousand impoverished spectators, all of whom were anxious for Williams, a native African raised in Cleveland, to defeat the 'Great White Hope'. At the conclusion of fifteen blood-soaked rounds, the judges were deadlocked, meaning that Williams would retain his title.

Nine months later, a rematch entitled the 'Bam Bam in the Sudan' was staged, with several bizarre timekeeping issues coming into play as Williams escaped the greatest pummeling of his life with yet another draw, much to the protest of international news sources and boxing experts worldwide.

Brickyard retired the following week, leaving the Heavyweight Title vacant for the first time in decades.

The fight to decide a new champion was to be held in Boston, and Fuerst was to face Jack 'Bombs Away!' Newcombe in a battle between the top two contenders for the greatest crown in professional sports.

Fuerst trained harder than he had ever trained before for his third title shot, and despite the death of Mad Dog just one month prior to the heavily-anticipated bout, Wolf was foaming at the mouth to destroy Newcombe and lay claim to his rightful place as undisputed king of the boxing world[18].

---

[18] From Wikipedia: A literary trope is the use of figurative language, via word, phrase or an image, for artistic effect such as using a figure of speech. The word trope has also come to be used for describing commonly recurring literary and rhetorical devices, motifs or clichés in creative works.

Now, standing over a bloodied, convulsing Bombs Away! midway through the first round of the nationally-televised fight, Fuerst sensed a powerful, godlike vitality pulsating through him, as if he was an omnipotent being standing before an assembly of trembling, groveling mortals.

Wolfgang felt, for the first time in his life, as if the world was truly his for the taking.

«««—»»»

When I leave my hotel room to head to the Silver Station I spot that couple I listened to banging and they're both ugly as hell. The woman weighs well over 300 pounds so now I feel gross for having masturbated to their vigorous love making session. I go back into my room and start washing my cock with hand soap but then I realize that that doesn't make sense, so I just put the whole thing out of my mind and depart for Riverdale. There's a big accident on the freeway so I kill time waiting for the meat wagon to arrive by doing some more reading.

CHAPTER VIII

Blanketed in thick, oppressive globules of mud, Heinrich Fuerst–aka Daniel B. Cooper–moved with impressive speed along the westernmost bank of the Columbia River, sweat pouring out of him like a raging geyser as he continued to run on pure adrenaline.

A heavy rain continued to assail the northwestern corner of the United States, helping to cover Fuerst's tracks as his dramatic escape continued unabated. He had successfully staged one of the most daring crimes in American history, yet it would be hours before he would be able to bask in the success of his ingenious plan.

Fuerst stopped momentarily to check his stainless-steel compass and adjust his path accordingly. His heart jackhammered against the two hundred thousand dollars in unmarked bills that were strapped tightly to his chest, the makeshift fastening device housing his ill-gotten fortune threatening to break free at the behest of his rowdy circulatory organ[19].

Since going AWOL from the army six months earlier, Fuerst had fallen on severely hard times, his identity

---

[19] From Wikipedia: *Bad English* is the self-titled platinum-selling debut album by American rock supergroup Bad English, released in 1989.

changing daily along with his location. After subsidizing his drifter's existence through petty, violent crimes, Heinrich had formulated a grand scheme that would afford him a comfortable existence as well as the funds necessary to reignite his father's dormant religion and establish a radical political organization of his very own, which he planned to call the United Aryan Front.

Having originally enlisted in the army as a paratrooper, Fuerst had undergone extensive training in skydiving. He had made dozens of successful jumps before transferring into mobile infantry. The devoted white supremacist had never imagined he would one day be using the knowledge provided to him by the U.S. Airborne Unit to jump from a Boeing 727 during poor weather conditions, but that was exactly what he had done earlier that evening, his destiny's 'seed money' now in tow.

As the plane he had hijacked made its way to Reno, Nevada, Fuerst again stopped to catch his breath, wiping the mud from his brow and crouching beneath an unusually thick water birch tree. His warm breath was suddenly visible beneath the provisional natural shelter he had deftly appropriated[20].

Reaching into his back right pants pocket, Fuerst pulled out the magazine he had read throughout the various flights he had travelled on whilst committing his soon-to-be-infamous crime—a recent copy of *Sporting World*. The cover of the popular publication featured a stern-looking, shirtless 'Furious' Wolfgang Fuerst flexing

---

[20] From Wikipedia: *Backlash*, is the second and final studio album by American AOR supergroup Bad English, released in 1991.

his massive bicep with a gold-and-jewel encased black belt hanging from his red-gloved hand. *Don't worry Brother—you too are a part of this… even if you do not yet realize it…*

European money launderers were set to accept the ten thousand twenty-dollar bills Fuerst knew full-well had been photographed on microfilm by government officials, the flagged cash set to be filtered through an elaborate chain of foreign networks. Heinrich would be left with roughly half of his earnings from the heist, a tidy sum to say the least; more than enough to get the proverbial ball rolling on his New World Order.

Shortly after Heinrich recommenced his arduous hike, a small campsite suddenly appeared before him. The newly-affluent fugitive quickly darted behind a sturdy birch tree, panting heavily. Through the rain he could see the focused glow of a flashlight dancing wildly within a blue, double skin tent. A badly rusted pickup truck was situated nearby. *What luck!*

Fuerst quickly drew an ash-handled puukko knife from his backpack and readied to get on with the task at hand. His dry mouth suddenly moistened as he salivated at the prospect of murdering a young family or, ideally, a teenaged couple skipping their curfew in order to enjoy a passionate love making session deep within the quiet, peaceful forest.

Traffic finally abates, and I end up pulling up to the Silver Station just after ten o'clock. The joint's an older-looking mansion—the kind of place a bald, crippled psychic might teach magic freaks how to use their powers for the betterment of society in. There's even ivy on the walls and shit.

I pull up to what looks like a main entrance and a couple of sentries—big, dark sunglasses—appear out of nowhere. Just as one of them taps on my window, another couple of guards—also big and also donning dark sunglasses—burst through the front doors with a young girl sandwiched between them. She's tiny but feisty, kicking and screaming as they escort her off of the premises, clearly against her will. "You can't do this!" she shrieks, adding something about freedom of the press as the two guards who'd been interested in me for a hot second go off to help their buddies deal with this crazy dame. Before they even get over there though the chick sprints away, out towards this massive, pristine, empty parking lot. She spits back towards the guards and the main entrance and then spots my idling sedan.

All of a sudden, she's in my passenger seat telling me to drive. The four gorilla-men take a second to make sure they all still look badass and then advance towards us. "Drive, asshole!" the broad yells. I don't know why but I listen to her, peeling out of the parking lot and back towards the highway as if she's a sorceress and I'm under her spell or something.

《《《———》》》

We're on the road for like five minutes before either one of us says anything. The sparkplug tells me her name's Kelly and I give her my real name in return. She's kind of cute in a punk rock/girlfriend-of-a-demented-supervillain kind of way, her short, loud hair and lithe frame automatically costing her a fair amount of points on the Shane Bishop Fuckability Scale. Well, not that many I guess actually.

She asks if I mind if she smokes and I tell her to go ahead and pollute our lungs since it's a free country and we're all gonna die in some shitty manner anyway. Then I ask what the hell happened back at the Silver Station as she rolls down her window and lights her cigarette. After taking a couple of drags she tells me her name is actually Jenny and she's not sure why she lied earlier. Then she asks me where we're going. Some asshole in a convertible cuts me off and I lay on the horn pretty heavy, calling the guy all kinds of awful names in Russian.

"Vy govorite russkiy?" Kelly/Jenny asks me. "Or only swear words?"

I catch myself laughing and ask my passenger if she's hungry. Turns out she is.

«‹‹——›››

We pull off the highway and hit up this rundown diner filled with a healthy mix of white trash and wetback clientele. Our waitress looks like she's about 13 months pregnant somehow and she takes forever to get us seated and set up with menus but because she's got a bun in the oven I can't short-change her on the tip or else I'll look like an asshole and shit. Fucking society.

Jenny looks like she hasn't eaten in about a month. She's got that 60s-London-fashion-model-devil-may-care-anorexia and/or 90s-Seattle-heroin-rockstar vibe going for her which I guess is pretty cool. Her tawny complexion and sexy-feline-like features make her exact age tough to determine but it's definitely somewhere in the 20s.

She catches me staring at her impossibly green eyes as she's studying the menu and tells me not to get any ideas because she's a lesbian. "That's cool," I hear myself say. "So, we've got that in common—we both like chicks."

"I guess," Jenny sighs, taking out her smartphone and scrolling absently through Chirrup[21]. "So, what's your story, dude?" she asks, continuing to read various chirps on her phone.

"That's kind of hard to explain. At least over breakfast anyway."

"What are you like a secret agent or something?" she snickers, possibly at her own question or at a humorous chirp she just read.

"Maybe. If I tell you I have to kill you though. Or at least wipe your mind with my fancy... mind... wiping... gadget."

Jenny puts her phone down and smiles at me flirtatiously, my heart skipping a beat. "Well we wouldn't want that now, would we?"

"What about you?" I ask, motioning for the waitress to bring us some coffee. "What's your story, kiddo?"

"Journalist. Trying to be anyway."

"Tough industry nowadays."

"It is."

The waitress reluctantly pours us our coffees and sneezes on our table as she asks us what we want. I tell her to just bring us two breakfast specials and some O.J. She waddles off, moaning loudly so as to elicit more sympathy and, I guess, increase her potential tip money. Whatever.

"So. Why were you at the Silver Station?" Jenny asks me. "You don't look or act like a Solarite?"

"You first, kiddo—what were you doing there? Why did those guards toss you out of the place like that?"

---

[21] Pastiche [pa-steesh, pah-] noun.
A literary, musical, or artistic piece consisting wholly or chiefly of motifs or techniques borrowed from one or more sources.

"Why do I have to go first?"

"Because I'm buying breakfast."

"Fair enough."

Jenny explains how she's been working on some big story about the Church and how they brainwash their members, including movie stars and wannabe movie stars like Iris. The editor at the pseudo-tabloid magazine Jenny works at—*STAR BEAT*—wanted her to go through the recruitment process for an exposé on the bizarre, celebrity-laden cult. It was the first feature she'd been assigned after a year of copy editing and producing mindless 'listicles'.

I ask her what a 'listicle' is and she looks at me like I'm senile and then gives a really condescending explanation. Fucking millennials.

"So, what happened when you went in to sign up for Brain-washing 101?" I ask, mimicking her condescension.

"This fell out of my jacket pocket when I was doing my Ecliptometer Test," she says, holding up a small digital recorder. "The guy I'd been dealing with freaked out and called security on me. And that's how I ended up meeting you, Shane Bishop."

It never really occurred to me how odd it was that she was so panicked and jumped in the car with me back at the Silver Station. It didn't seem like all that a dangerous situation, no more than being kicked out of a movie theater for talking too loudly, making fun of fat kids in an arcade or giving yourself a cocaine enema in the lobby of a nice hotel at least.

"The Church is bad news, man, who knows what they would've done to me..." There's a look of modest fear in Jenny's eyes and I guess I don't really know much about these Solarite fuckers other than what I've seen on TV and shit, so I ask her to give me the lowdown on the Church.

"Not so fast, Daddio," she says, her perky flirtatiousness returning with a vengeance. "You have to tell me what you were doing at Solarite HQ this morning first."

Our waitress brings us over our meals and the food looks terrible, but the portions are huge! What a country!

I pour some ketchup on to my scrambled eggs and tell Jenny that I'm pretty sure that my daughter joined the Church last week after being recruited from a bullshit acting class and has since disappeared.

"That doesn't surprise me." Jenny snaps a piece of crispy bacon in half and dunks it in her coffee before eating it. "They've been recruiting like crazy lately for some reason."

"What have you dug up on them so far?" I ask. "For your story I mean."

Jenny spreads some apple jelly onto a piece of toast and starts telling me that the Church was originally founded by some science fiction writer in Wisconsin in the 60s and then it resurfaced here in California at some point in the 80s. "They're basically just new age sun worshippers," she explains. "A bunch of Pagan-like mumbo jumbo from what I can tell."

The part about the science fiction writer from Wisconsin obviously sounds familiar but I push it out of my mind for the moment. "What makes them so dangerous then?" I ask.

"There's all kinds of rumors about them sacrificing virgins, killing off dissenters and whatnot," Jenny whispers, semi-dramatically.

"So why risk going in there like that? Has to be an easier way to get the story, right?"

Jenny shrugs and eats another stick of bacon. "Gotta start somewhere," she says. "Would've been fine if I hadn't dropped my stupid recorder."

"So now what?" I ask.

She slides the digital recorder across the table and an eerily seductive smile makes its way across her gaunt face[22]. "Maybe we can help each other out," she says. "Do you have any experience infiltrating evil organizations, Shane Bishop?"

"As a matter of fact... I do indeed."

《《《—》》》

We pull back into the Silver Station parking lot and Jenny tells me she'll wait in the car since she's been red flagged by the Church and whatnot. "What if they recognize me as your getaway driver from this morning?" I ask.

"Well then we're screwed."

Fucking millennials.

"What's this test they make recruits do? Econo-something?"

"Ecliptometer. It's some weird thing they strap you into and then they ask you questions. I didn't make it to the question part."

"Questions about what?"

"What did I just say?"

"Touché. Well. Wish me luck I guess."

"Good luck I guess."

《《《—》》》

I climb the Church's stairs and open its main doors. A mega-opulent atrium greets me, the floors made out of expensive-looking marble. A bunch of classicalish sculptures are all over the place. Before I can take it all in a couple of overeager

---

[22] From Wikipedia: Risus sardonicus or rictus grin is a highly characteristic, abnormal, sustained spasm of the facial muscles that appears to produce grinning.

recruitment agents—a dude and a chick—sprint up to me and introduce themselves.

The guy—young, high cheekbones, neatly combed blonde hair, soft blue eyes—and his female companion—30ish, petite, pale, her dark hair cut into a stylish bob, her outfit snug but not too revealing—step over one another both literally and figuratively as they accost me in the Church's grand foyer. "Good afternoon, friend!" the dude near-exclaims as he reaches in to shake my hand. I oblige him and then the broad wants to shake my hand too which is an acceptable course of action given the circumstances I suppose.

"Welcome to the Church of Solarism," they say in unison. "And congratulations on taking your first step along the path to self-fulfillment!"

I give each of these characters a slow, deliberate once-over and remove a nonexistent toothpick from my mouth. "Thanks," I growl, tossing the invisible toothpick to the ground. "Where do I sign up for this… religion?"

My new friends laugh mockingly and tell me that becoming a member of the Church is a "complex and beautiful process" that will change my life forever. They seem to believe it. Wholeheartedly.

"I can personally attest to the immense power contained within these walls." The pretty boy doofus puts his arm around my shoulder and directs me towards a corridor on the far side of the atrium. "I myself was once a lost soul, addicted to reefer and prostitutes, but the Church has put me on the path to salvation and now I have a fruitful existence overflowing with happiness and spiritual fulfillment. It all began in this very building, in these very halls—a journey you are invited to join us in, mister?"

"Jones. Jimmy Jones."

"Very nice to meet you, Jimmy!" the woman says. "My name is Tanya and this is my husband Tania."

"Yeah, okay, it's uh…nice to meet you guys too." We pass a huge fish tank on our way to wherever we're going and there are all kinds of crazy neon fish swimming around in there and I'm pretty sure I see that same miniature dragon I killed in the opening chapter among them, but I guess it could just be his cousin or something.

Tanya and Tania lead me down a vast, sterile corridor—into a small room that appears to contain only an old school video monitor and a cold, metallic chair. The walls are medium grey and ominously plain-looking.

"Before your personality assessment is administered we'd like to show you a brief introductory video which gives you a bit of background about the Church of Solarism," the husband and wife team proclaim, again in unison. Weirdos.

They walk up over to the monitor and I get a good look at Tanya's healthy, firm ass as she bends over to start the recording. Tania catches me ogling his wife but what the fuck is this pansy gonna do about it?[23]

The couple beams out of the room and then the video begins playing: a black solar wheel slowly rotates on the screen as strange, ambient music becomes faintly audible. I start to feel dizzy and a flash of panic tells me to get the hell out of dodge, but I'm pinned to my chair by some kind of invisible force field… The melodic, angelic voice of a hot-sounding woman begins to speak as the wheel continues to spin, clockwise[24].

"Throughout human history nearly every great civilization, religion, and culture… has focused on the prodigious, awe-

---

[23] Nothing! That's what!

[24] From Wikipedia: A clockwise (typically abbreviated as CW) motion is one that proceeds in the same direction as a clock's hands: from the top to the right, then down and then to the left, and back up to the top.

75

inspiring power of the sun as a basis for worship... This is of course exceedingly logical, as it is the sun that makes life on earth possible, provides us with heat, air, all of the basic necessities for existence... All the while however, the true power of the sun has gone unnoticed... until now." *What the hell is this shit?* I notice I've been holding my breath, so I stop doing that and start breathing–the process that moves air in and out of the lungs, allowing the diffusion of oxygen and carbon dioxide to and from the external environment into and out of the blood–but the air I take in tastes funny or maybe it doesn't.

"In Ancient Greece, they worshiped Helios... In Rome, it was Sol Invictus... The Egyptians gave the highest of reverence to Ra, the all-powerful deity who knew no peer... Svarog was the supreme god-creator in Slavic mythology, while the Hindus worship the benevolent healer of Surya..." With each idol the voice references, its corresponding symbol is projected upon the screen. A constellation-esque pattern is soon encircling the constantly-rotating solar wheel I'm staring at.

"Odin, the chief god in Norse mythology... the bringer of life itself to the Nordic peoples... was used as inspiration in the work of Baron Carl von Reichenbach in the nineteenth century as he produced undeniable scientific evidence of a unifying vital energy which he dubbed the 'Odic Force'... a very real frequency that has connected all living things since the dawn of time..."

A black and white photograph of a serious-looking, white-haired gentleman in his early-60s now occupies the center of the screen. Pretty ugly dude. 'Pretty ugly' is an oxymoron, right?[25]

"Baron von Reichenbach was a prophet who synthesized the very essence of existence in his scientific experiments, giving us

---

[25] Sure.

the ability to transcend our physical barriers and experience cosmic ecstasy while still on earth..."

Caesura.

"Unfortunately, most of von Reichenbach's work was destroyed following his death in 1869, and it was not until the second half of the twentieth century when our magnanimous leader... Reginald Tilden... the founder of the Church of Solarism... discovered some of the Baron's old notebooks at an auction while vacationing in Germany... An accomplished philosopher as well as a popular science fiction and fantasy author, Tilden was able to continue on with the experiments of von Reichenbach, jointly utilizing the varied rituals of every civilization's sun worship to tap into the Odic Force. By piecing together the various elements of all of history's great empires and their solar deities, Tilden was able to assemble the principles which now comprise the religion known as Solarism... Those who join the ranks of this awe-inspiring faith, which transcends the barriers of all traditional ecclesiastical groups, are able to achieve a visceral nirvana compared to which all other joys can be deemed trivial, meaningless..."

A color photograph of a jovial, robust man is now being broadcast onto the video monitor in both recruitment booths. I guess it's that Tilden guy. *That name sounds familiar, doesn't it?*[26]

"As the power of the Odic Force is indeed great, one cannot experience it without taking the proper steps to ready oneself for the earth shattering cosmic might of the all-encompassing energy

---

[26] mei·o·sis (mī-ō′sĭs)
   n. pl. mei·o·ses
   A. Genetics The process of cell division in sexually reproducing organisms that reduces the number of chromosomes from diploid to haploid, as in the production of gametes.
   B. Rhetorical understatement.
   C. None of the Above
   D. All of the Above

field... Therefore, the great secrets of Solarism cannot be revealed to those who have not properly readied themselves to undergo a complete spiritual metamorphosis... There are, naturally, steps one must take on the path to eternal bliss, as one must ready one's self to be able to channel the Odic Force through one's physical being... If one should attempt to tap into the force too soon, their soul would become inverted and their life energy would become trapped in a permanent purgatory, never able to break free from the shackles of spiritual imprisonment—a black hole of desolation in which no light can exist..."

Another caesura.

"The simple yet profound goal of the Church of Solarism is to prepare our members to be able to channel the Odic Force through their individual life vessels and be a part of the universal energy field that makes existence possible... To accomplish this, you need to progress through the prescribed stages along the Plane of Luminosity, which was developed by Reginald Tilden shortly after he'd founded the Church... It is only by following these steps that you can develop your spiritual consciousness to the point where you are able to fulfill your destiny and achieve ethereal transcendence, profound serenity, and ultimately... immortality, as perpetual reincarnation is the end result of harnessing the Odic Force... Each set of stages on the Plane are modified to suit your individual needs as per the results of your Ecliptometer test, which you will now undergo as part of your introduction to the Church of Solarism... your admission into a new, vibrant life, and an eternal, brilliant happiness that you will carry with you for all of time."

The video stops. The door opens up and the tension that's been assailing me quickly dissipates, which is nice. Some scientician-looking dude is suddenly in the room and he's got a shiny metal contraption under his arm. It's about the size of a small microwave.

Mr. Science Man introduces himself as 'Fred' and proceeds to strap a Velcro-laced band around my right arm. I'm wearing a golf shirt so it's a pretty quick process. Fred plugs the bright green wire protruding from the arm band into the metal box doohickey and starts fiddling with some black dials while humming the melody of a faggy show tune that I can't quite place.

The box starts to make some beeping sounds and the white-coated dork starts explaining that he's going to ask me—'the subject'—a series of questions designed to determine where I'm to be slotted along the Plane of Luminosity should I decide to join The Church.

"It's like a lie detector or something?" I ask.

"No," Fred laughs. "Not at all—it's simply designed to gauge certain aspects of your personality. We have different categories and levels that correspond to the given individual characteristics of our given members. Not everyone is the same and thus the Plane has unique traits, just as humanity does."

"Okay," I tell the guy. "Let's do it I guess."

Fred smiles, widely. "Please state your full name."

"James Warren Jones."

"How old are you?"

"Forty-eight."

"In what city were you born?"

"Hoboken, New Jersey."

"Have you ever made an offhand comment about a friend or coworker that you later regretted?"

"Uh, yeah, I guess so…"

"Please answer only with a 'yes' or 'no' from now on, James."

"Sorry, Freddy."

"That's fine. Now. Tell me…have you ever looked through an encyclopedia or thesaurus for entertainment purposes?"

"Yes."

"Do you ever feel confused or anxious about your path in life?"

"Yes."

"Have you ever been afraid of something that it is illogical to be afraid of?"

"No."

"Do you ever worry about your financial stability?"

"Yes."

"Have you ever felt apprehensive in an unfamiliar social setting?"

"Yes."

"Do you ever feel concerned for your safety when riding in an elevator?"

"No."

After a few minutes of this bullshit questioning, it's finally time to hear the results of my Ecliptometer Test. Oh, goody.

"Well, Mr. Jones, I'm happy to say that you're definitely in the right place," Fred tells me. "Your personality is classified as Level Four Neopolysmic, a not uncommon classification for a man your age. Should you decide to join The Church and partake in our next initiation ceremony, you will most definitely be able to attain Stage Nine Luminosity by your sixtieth birthday."

I'm daydreaming about slutty cheerleaders in this softcore porno I watched this one time and not really registering what this dipshit is telling me. "Huh? Oh, thanks… That's swell—I always thought I might be… neo… poly…septic…"

"Neopolysmic."

"That too."

A healthy amount of impressive-sounding gibberish and jargon comes out of my auditor's mouth as he further expounds upon the details of this particular personality classification. Meanwhile, the slutty cheerleaders in my mind's eye are doing all kinds of nasty shit to each other, breaking out some kinky toys and whatnot.

"So, what are the membership fees at this place?" I ask, snapping back into character and getting down to business.

"Excuse me?" Fred asks, doing a decent job of feigning pseudo-offense.

"You know... membership in this thing, what would it cost me if I signed up?"

"We would never dream of *charging* our fellow spiritual devotees... It is one hundred percent free to join the Church of Solarism."

I'm pretty sure this is a bogus claim based on what we know about the Church's real-life counterpart, but it doesn't really matter since all I really need to know is what the next step is to join since that's probably where Iris is at now. And I guess Jenny needs it too, for her story or whatever.

"What's the process for joining the Church officially then?" I unfasten the arm band and toss it on top of the metal box.

"Well, all of our new members attend an initiation retreat at one of our spiritual fulfillment centers. There are several throughout the country."

"Where's the one you'd send me if I joined the Church right here, right now?" My tone is a little more forceful than I guess it should've been and Fred starts to look at me funny, like he might know I've got another agenda here.

"I... We can discuss that in the conference room," Fred stammers as he starts to make his way towards the door. I stand up and grab Fred by the throat, nearly crushing his windpipe as I slam him against the wall. "Where?" I snarl. "Where will they send me next if I sign up for this bullshit."

Fred's eyes are bursting with fear and he tries to flail against the wall for a few seconds until he wisely decides to play ball and starts trying to talk. I loosen my grip and he gasps frantically while he tells me that the closest retreat takes place on a farm just outside of Barstow. I punch the guy in the stomach just for good measure and then those same security guards from this morning burst through the door and rough me up pretty good before tossing me out of the joint. I realize I could've just gone to the retreat instead of snapping on Fred right as one hits me with a solid right cross which I guess gives credence to that old idiom about 'knocking sense' into people.

《《《——》》》

Jenny looks freaked out when I open the car door and she sees my battered face. She asks me what the hell happened, and I tell her that we're going to Barstow, but she needs to drive since I'm seeing double at the moment and probably have a concussion.

"We should probably stop at a drug store first though," I add, wiping some blood from my mouth as I hand her back her audio recorder. "Pick up a few things. Licorice and what not."

《《《——》》》

We pull into a chain pharmacy and the car we park next to looks like something out of a Saturday morning cartoon about turbocharged nukemobiles. The body is a bright, almost neon, shade of orange and the tires look like they're made out of tanned rhinoceros hide. A humongous spoiler adorns the monstrosity's rear end while the front bumper appears to be affixed with a steampunk-style cold fusion generator purchased via the mail order catalogue of a mad scientist from a 1950s b-movie.

I nod to the funky car's leather-clad owner as we pass each other at the store's entrance/exit and he mumbles something in a foreign language I'm not familiar with prior to unleashing a high-pitched battle cry, sprinting behind his ride's steering wheel and peeling off like a bat out of hades. So that was weird. Jenny doesn't seem to notice the whole thing which is also pretty goddamn weird.

The lighting in the drug store is a tad on the dark side and the aisles don't look like they've been cleaned in a decade or two but I'm able to find the bandage/antiseptic section easy enough, so I grab a healthy mix of products off the shelf while a random dog wandering the store sits and watches me silently. Jenny goes off to get some chocolate milk from the fridge designated as containing dairy products and then after she takes out a half-gallon carton of her favorite brand she has an impassioned discussion about physics and philosophy with a female clerk for a while[27].

On my way to the checkout I pass a rack of discounted paperback novels and notice a copy of WAVEFRONT by Reginald Tilden for sale. There's a tingling sensation along the back of my neck that I haven't felt for a while as I pick the book up and flip to a random spot near the back and start reading...

---

[27] From Wikipedia: The Bechdel test (/ˈbɛkdəl/ BEK-dəl) asks whether a work of fiction features at least two women who talk to each other about something other than a man.

WAVEFRONT

CHAPTER 69

Gripping a surging electroton between his sweaty palms, Optio Second Class Badyn Taylor peered over a pile of corpses to see an enemy legion advancing with tremendous rapidity. They would overtake his post within a matter of minutes, the bloody battleground stretching out for miles around him littered with fallen members of the Dominion's Armed Forces.

"What do we do now, sir?" a frightened teenager under Taylor's command asked, his timbre overflowing with desperation.

"I guess we surrender." Taylor deactivated his electroton and pulled a white flag out of his utility pouch. He choked back a potent rage that had been simmering within him for months as his primal instinct for survival now guided his actions.

"What will happen to us?" the smooth-faced boy inquired, fear clearly coursing through every fiber of his being.

"Prison. Torture. That's if they take us alive mind you," Taylor caustically replied, trying not to think about the stories he'd heard about Nadiri labor camps.

"Verp that!" a badly-wounded maniple exclaimed, propping himself up with a makeshift crutch and unleashing a deafening battle cry as he charged out of the bunker towards their enemies, discharging his electroton wildly in the direction of the Nadiris as he staggered along the arid farmland.

Taylor looked away just as a plasma blast struck the glory-seeking soldier squarely in the chest, blowing him to pieces. A heavy silence fell upon the scene.

"You know I enlisted in the army because of you," another young soldier at Taylor's side stated contritely. "You were my hero."

"Sorry about that, kid," Taylor replied, fixing the white flag onto a long pole they'd discovered in a neighboring village the previous afternoon. After the flag was securely fastened to the pole, he placed it on the ground and produced a silver flask from the inside pocket of his uniform, a gift from a fan during his first season with the Peltasts. Taylor unscrewed the container's lid and tilted his head backwards as he poured several ounces of abis down his throat, the flavorless liquor fleetingly warming his innards.

Taylor tossed the flask aside as he readied to surrender to the Nadiris, cursing the Dominion under his breath as he stood hesitantly. He raised the flag high for their adversaries to see. Within seconds a dozen enemy soldiers were pointing their glowing cylindrical weapons at Taylor's cohort. All four surviving members of Unit 421 had their arms raised in the air as their imposing captors yelped unintelligible commands at them in the coarse language of the north.

"Too bad you weren't a trigon fan, eh kid?" Taylor coldly offered to the trembling youngster who'd imprudently followed him into the army.

"Yeah," the ill-fated maniple replied, tersely. "Too bad."

«‹‹——»»›

"What the hell took you so long?!" Jenny demands when I get back to the rental car. I guess she paid for her chocolate milk when I wasn't looking and left without me at some point in time preceding our current interaction.

"Sorry," I say. "Got caught up in a book."

"A fucking book? Are you serious?"

"Why would I joke about that?"

"I don't know dude, you're obviously pretty unbalanced."

"No argument there." I tell Jenny I'm fine to drive which is more or less true and she slides over into the passenger seat as I get behind the wheel, fire up the engine and drive out of the parking lot.

"How long of a drive is it to Barstow?" I ask.

"Couple of hours I guess." Jenny is messing around on her smartphone and starts giggling at something she reads.

"Do me a favor," I say flatly, my mind racing at the existence of WAVEFRONT in this dimension. "Grab that zPad-looking thing in the back and open the LiveStory app."

"Um, okay." Jenny unfastens her seatbelt and stretches back to retrieve the tablet from the backseat, giving me a glimpse of her firm, toned midriff that I allow myself to evolve into an outright leer that quite nearly causes me to swerve into another lane.

"What happened?!" Jenny demands as she thrusts herself back into her seat, tablet in hand, shortly after I narrowly avoid a slow-moving pickup truck and hammer the rental car's horn a few times.

"Bastard cut me off," I say.

"What is this thing anyway?" Jenny asks, our brush with death barely registering with her.

"A magic computer tablet I bought off of a Russian wizard."

She snickers but then she sees I'm not joking. "Okay, so what's this 'LiveStory' app then? Never heard of it."

"Can you just read from it for a bit? I've got a bad feeling about something."

"Alright, whatever. Gotta pass the time somehow I guess."

She clears her throat and starts reading to me...

CHAPTER IX

Grinning curiously at an old folder which contained the successful application forms for both Heinrich and Wolfgang Fuerst, Head Master Axmann sat behind his pristine marble desk, awaiting the arrival of the most capable pupil he had encountered since founding his underground institute for aspiring Nazis several years earlier[28].

Upon somehow managing to escape both the Führerbunker and World War II with his life, Axmann had served nearly four years in prison for his alleged crimes against humanity. The former Hitler Youth leader had used his time in Allied custody effectively–planning the curriculum he would implement at what would become the Academy of National Socialist Advancement.

After faking his own death shortly after being released from prison, Axmann had approached several affluent ex-Nazis with his idea of forming a small boarding school which would be able to educate members of the post-Reich generation on the tenants of National Socialism. The school's aim would be to have its grads infiltrate

---

[28] From Wikipedia: Run-on sentences occur when two or more independent clauses are joined without using a coordinating conjunction (i.e., for, and, nor, but, or, yet, so) or correct punctuation (i.e., semicolons, dashes, or periods).

various bureaucratic agencies so as to one day stage a coup and reclaim the Fatherland for their own.

It had taken little effort for Axmann to procure the funds necessary to purchase an aging farmhouse in Gelsenkirchen and convert it into a functional school, dozens of former SS members volunteering to serve as teachers at the clandestine educational center. The list of applicants was much greater, and the Academy quickly became a much talked about entity within aristocratic neo-Nazi social circles. The honor of becoming one of 'Axmann's Apprentices' was immediately deemed great, the school's reputation soon spreading like wild fire throughout the neo-fascist underworld.

For over twenty years Axmann and his hand-selected ex-Nazis had educated their pupils in the ways of National Socialism, with each graduate going onto gain employment within the West German civil service. Every branch of the nation's government had been infiltrated by Axmann's protégés, and the targeted date of their impending coup, to be carried out jointly with the postwar National Socialist organization Die Spinne, was now a mere seven years away.

Die Spinne's elaborate network of former SS officers constantly pushed Axmann to accept more students at the Academy, but he steadfastly refused, preferring to only take in those he himself deemed fit for the most important mission in the history of the Aryan Race. Now one month removed from his sixtieth birthday, Axmann had aged remarkably well considering his trying adolescence and early adulthood. The one-time Reichsleiter was consumed at all times by the task of readying the perspective leaders of the Fourth Reich for their noble crusade, the future glories of his people constantly occupying prime real estate at the forefront of his twisted mind.

While he had often battled demonic doubts regarding the Aryan destiny throughout his tenure as the Academy's Headmaster, Axmann now held in his one remaining hand a letter from the United States that offered much in the way of consecration for his cause.

International expansion had oft been discussed by the Academy's Board of Directors along with Die Spinne's chief administrators. No viable conduit with any foreign agency had ever been established however. Until now.

A light tapping on his office door prompted Axmann to invite Declan Farrelly, that year's Academy valedictorian, to enter the fanciful, neatly-decorated office in which he spent the majority of his time.

Walking into a room bursting with subdued grandeur, Farrelly marveled at the collection of Third Reich paraphernalia that his Headmaster had on display. Medals, helmets, uniforms, photographs, and various other remnants of Germany's golden era proliferated throughout the crowded workspace. A large architectural etching of Germania adorned the wall behind Axmann's brown leather throne chair.

Sitting down to face his leader, Farrelly could see the signature of Adolph Hitler clearly written in the bottom right corner of the impressive pencil sketch, which was to have been the blueprint for a Utopian society that would have defined the 20th century had the cursed Allies not emerged victorious from the Second World War.

A stern-looking, athletic boy in his late teens, Farrelly had been sent to study with Axmann by his uncle Terry after a car accident had orphaned the precocious adolescent five years earlier. Terry Farrelly had aided Irish Republican Army President Sean Russell and the Nazis in the planning of Operation Green in 1940, a botched mission which would have seen the Axis invade the British Isles with Ireland as a landing ground and with the support of several battalions of IRA soldiers.

Having narrowly escaped capture on several occasions, Terry Farrelly had been living in an IRA Safe House in Dublin when he had received news of his brother and sister-in-law's fatal accident, his young nephew being targeted for placement in a British orphanage—a fate worse than death in the fanatical revolutionary's opinion.

Making use of his extensive list of radical associates, Terry had then arranged for Declan to be rescued and brought to his hideout. For six months the exceptionally bright orphan was educated in the ways of guerilla military tactics, accompanying his uncle on several terrorist missions while learning to hate the British and cultivating a healthy distrust of everyone else while in the company of the IRA's most nefarious faction[29].

Terry had heard about Axman's Academy while on a mission to buy unused Nazi munitions which had been abandoned in a subterranean warehouse in the Hurtgen Forrest after the U.S. Army had overtaken the area in late 1944. The gentleman with whom he had negotiated the deal, an eccentric fellow named Hochbichler, had sent his

---

[29] From Wikipedia: "Information dump" is the term given for overt exposition, which writers want to avoid.

own son to learn the ways of Nazism at The Academy and had nothing but great things to say about the program Axmann and his disciples had developed in their quest to mold the next generation of National Socialists into intelligent, devoted officers of the Aryan cause.

The very next week Declan was in Gelsenkirchen, sharing a tiny dorm room with an Italian boy named Leccisi who was very much there against his will, at the extreme behest of his relatives who had founded a neo-fascist league in southern Europe known as Alto Nazional.

Leccisi's reluctance to devote himself to his studies eventually led to a severe beating by one of his teachers, the injuries he endured leading directly to his death a few days later. Farrelly was then forced to room with the obnoxious, dimwitted heir to an American real estate empire for the duration of his stay at The Academy, a tenure which had proven to be amazingly successful. The Irishman had received the highest marks of any student the school had ever housed, also excelling at the military and sporting exercises the student body would partake in on weekends.

With his graduation only a few days away, Farrelly assumed that Headmaster Axmann had summoned him to his office to inform him which West German neo-Nazi organization he would be joining upon his receipt of a swastika-clad diploma, and which agency of government he would be infiltrating under the guise of gainful employment.

"It will be a bittersweet moment for me Declan, your graduation from this institution," Axmann bemoaned, pouring two glasses of brandy from a bottle he'd produced from a cabinet adjacent to his desk. For a man with one arm, he was remarkably adept at tasks such as this.

"How do you mean, Sir?" Farrelly asked.

"You're quite simply the best student we've ever produced. Your aptitude for National Socialist ideology is truly remarkable—your military prowess and athletic abilities equally impressive..."

"Thank you, it has been an honor to have studied under a great man such as yourself these last few years."

"Yes, yes, your gratitude is not needed Herr Farrelly, but thank you for your kind words nonetheless." Axmann handed Farrelly his drink.

After toasting to the Führer at exactly 4:20pm—Hitler's birthday having been April 20—the two men drank from their crystal chalices. Extravagant self-satisfaction beamed through both Nazis as they continued their discussion.

"You are of course aware of the many leagues we have operating throughout West Germany at present, Herr Farrelly?"

"Of course, I very much look forward to joining whichever organization you see fit upon my impending graduation."

"Well I'm afraid we have different plans for you, son."

"Sir?"

"Last week I received a letter from a man living in America. He and his brother were meant to have studied here many years ago but were unable to due to... unforeseen circumstances... At any rate, he has founded an organization with aims very similar to our own in the United States and has requested that I aid his new group by sending my best student from this year's class to join him as he orchestrates what he promises to be an underground network of Aryan fascists as elaborate and great as our own – perhaps even more so."

Farrelly was both captivated by Axmann and wary of the words he spoke. He had been taught that America was nothing but a cesspool of oppressive Jewry and Negroid culture—a nation of weakness which had risen to prominence only at the behest of the Zionist agenda.

His duty overcoming his apprehension, Farrelly quickly accepted his fate.

"What is this man's name?" he asked.

"His name is Heinrich Fuerst... You are to meet him at New York's LaGuardia Airport on the morning of the eighteenth. Once in America you are to provide full administrative and logistical support for Herr Fuerst. You are to follow his every order, Declan... He has outlined a rather compelling plan for establishing a new Reich in the United States, with Germany ultimately falling under its rule once the Soviet Union inevitably falls and a Pan-Aryan Empire stretches across the globe."

Axmann paused, allowing Farrelly to take in the information he had provided.

"While we are officially confident that by decade's end we will be able to effectively retake control of our own government, I often doubt the legitimacy of this aim, Herr Farrelly. I fear that it may be several generations before National Socialism again reigns supreme in the annals of global politics, long after my time on this planet has come to an end I'm afraid..."

"Your devotion to future generations of National Socialists is truly noble, Headmaster."

"Well the most glorious political and movement in human history must be kept alive by someone, mustn't it?"

"Yes, of course sir, yours is the most noble and important of contributions our glorious cause has yet recorded."

"Right... well I was initially skeptical of Herr Fuerst's request. But after careful deliberation I have decided that it is indeed for the good of the Aryan cause that you do aid him in his quest to stage a fascist uprising in the... 'New World', as they once said."

"I look forward to using my training to great effect in the United States, Herr Axmann."

"Yes... Well my boy, I wish you the best of luck in America. I look forward to hearing of your progress in the coming years. I'm sure you and Herr Fuerst will be toasting to the successful installation of Aryan Supremacy in... New York's Time's Square in the near future."

The men shook hands and Declan departed, leaving Axmann alone once again. Alone with his thoughts. Alone with his memories. Alone with his madness[30].

Axmann destroyed the Fuerst brothers' Academy applications along with Farrelly's student file immediately once he had heard of Declan's successful arrival in New York, anxious to avoid any meddling by the Board of Directors in the matter. The very next day however, Axmann's office was raided by famed Nazi hunter Simon Liebermann, his entire network of German neo-Nazi agitators soon being captured as well. Die Spinne also crumbled as an unprecedented number of post-

---

[30] overwrite \ ˌō-vər-ˈrīt , ˌō-və- \
    transitive verb
    to write over the surface of
    to write in inflated or overly elaborate style

Nuremberg War Crime arrests were made nationwide[31].

Dozens of Academy graduates, some of whom had reached a level of extreme prominence in West German society, were ultimately jailed, their elaborate plot revealed by a ravenous international media contingent. One of the only Academy graduates to escape the wrath of the authorities was safely living in America as his former master was crucified by world opinion.

By the time he read of Axmann's execution in *Globe Magazine*, Declan Farrelly had already fallen under the spell of his new master—Heinrich Fuerst, future Führer of the Fourth Reich.

«« —»»

"This is terrible," Jenny moans as she looks up from the tablet and shoots me a nastyish look. "Who the hell wrote this thing—it might be the worst prose I've ever read in my entire life!"

"Technically the computer program is writing it," I say. "But we can give it guidelines for what we want the plot to be."

"Can we fix the writing? It's seriously atrocious, even for a computer. Not even Patterson and Brown are this insufferable!"

"Whatever Hipster Girl, can you just keep reading?"

"I'm not a hipster!"

"How is it that no one ever admits to being a hipster and yet they're everywhere? I'm an asshole, I'll readily admit to that. And we're everywhere too."

---

[31] From Wikipedia: Historical fiction is a literary genre in which the plot takes place in a setting located in the past. Historical fiction can be an ambiguous term: frequently it is used as a synonym for describing the historical novel; however, the term can be applied to works in other narrative formats, such as those in the performing and visual arts like theatre, opera, cinema, television, comics, and graphic novels.

"Oh, don't worry—I'm aware… What's this book got to do with the Solarites anyway?"

"I'm not sure. Maybe nothing. Maybe everything…"

"Jesus, is the computer telling you what to say now too, Shane?"

"Just read, Honey. Just read."

"Don't call me 'Honey.'" Jenny sighs and starts reading from the enchanted tablet again…

CHAPTER X

A nearly-beautiful young woman was putting the finishing touches on the Champ's makeup as a pair of surly teamsters fiddled with the lighting and the sound engineer yelled something about the boom mic being too close to the host.

Patty Winters checked her mascara one last time on her pocket mirror, her latest exclusive primetime interview special set to commence in thirty seconds[32].

"Everything good, Donny?" she asked of her producer, a hard-nosed live television veteran prone to profanity-laced fits of rage should anything interfere with a flawless broadcast. Patty Winters had hand-selected him to produce this, her greatest, most high-profile triumph to date for just this very reason. *Just wait until I cut into this Neanderthal! He won't see it coming!*

"Yeah, we're good Miss Winters. All set, Champ?" Donny asked, looking up from his clipboard to see an enormous thumb raised high in the air. The wide, toothy smile of Wolfgang Fuerst let him know that the mission was indeed set for takeoff.

---

[32] From Wikipedia: In a work of media adapted from a real or fictional narrative, a composite character is a character based on more than one individual.

The crew scurried from out of the makeshift set which had been erected in Wolf's cavernous trophy room. Donny raised his left arm and proclaimed, "Ten seconds people!"

Patty Winters made some last second adjustments to her outfit–a three-piece navy-blue pantsuit with a long-sleeve open shimmer jacket and a matching scoopneck camisole–as Wolfgang continued to broadcast his famous grin, breathing in deeply just so he could catch his interviewer sneaking furtive glances at his bulging pectorals. He looked like a caricature of masculinity–thick muscles bulging from every inch of his body as a several-sizes-too-small white sweater appeared to be on the verge of being ripped open with each breath he took.

"You look very nice, Patty," Fuerst stated plainly. His compliment was met with an icy, inhospitable stare as a countdown began: "five… four… three…"

Patty Winters sprang to life as a bright orange light did likewise atop the camera nearest her: "Good evening, and welcome to another Patty Winters Special. I'm your host, Patty Winters, and tonight I'll be speaking with Heavyweight Boxing Champion Wolfgang Fuerst from inside his palatial estate in Las Vegas, Nevada. How are you tonight, Champ?"

Fuerst leaned forward slightly, the extended drafting chair in which he sat creaking gently as the behemoth of a man shifted his weight. He paused, briefly, before saying: "I'm just wonderful Patty, thanks for taking the time to visit with me."

"Now I've got to tell you, sitting here in this… castle you've built here in the desert, with your Olympic medal, title belt, and various other trophies surrounding us, I've got to say, this really seems like the embodiment of the American dream."

"Yes, thank you Patty, I've worked hard to achieve my goals and it's definitely nice to be able to enjoy the fruits of my labor here in the great state of Nevada."

"A long way from the small town in Wisconsin where you grew up." Fuerst nodded at Patty Winters' statement. "And even farther from the nation of Austria, where you were in fact born in 1944 along with your twin brother Heinrich."

Wolfgang had, famously, rarely discussed his child-hood in public, and he could tell simply by Patty Winters' tone that this would not be the innocuous interview his handlers had been promised. Nonetheless, he obliged the newly-popular television journalist and delved into his murky personal history.

"Yes… My family is originally from a municipality known as Vichtenstein, which is in the district of Schärding in Upper Austria," he lied, effortlessly. He had recounted the fabricated tale so often among friends and business associates that it had become the functional truth, the sinister nature of his lineage an incredibly well-kept secret. "My mother died when I was still an infant. My father brought both my brother and myself to America at the end of the war to begin a new life."

"And during the war your father… served in the German Army, under the Nazis? Is that correct?"

Wolfgang never allowed his emotions to overcome him, his recent training with Tibetan monks having taught him to channel his anger into positive outlets. Now however, as he watched a smirking, arrogant reporter begin her assault of his past, he felt his blood begin to boil.

"No, that's not correct actually, Miss Winters. My father was a member of the military police in Austria, and, thank God, he never had to take part in any actual fighting. The war was an awful experience for my family, and I'm eternally grateful that my father was able to survive and was brave enough to bring his children to a great country such as this, where he knew our dreams could be fulfilled..."

The judges gave Round One to Fuerst. Patty Winters collected herself and readied for her next attack.

"Right, and your dreams have clearly all come true, Champ."

"Yes, I'm a lucky man."

"Now, getting back to your brother, Heinrich... He was the valedictorian of your high school, yet he ultimately enlisted in the army during the early days of the Vietnam War... Using a false identity no less... Is that correct, Wolf?"

What's she up to now?

"Yes, I was very proud of my brother's decision to fight for a country that has given my family so much. In addition to being a bona fide academic genius he was an incredibly devoted American—a true patriot who was willing to do anything for the country that he loved so very much. He probably used a fake name when enlisting to avoid the kind of discrimination which has plagued those of us with Germanic-sounding surnames for decades, a prejudice which would certainly be more pronounced in the military, Patty. Heinrich's courage was truly inspiring and I miss him dearly."

"So, your brother was killed in the line of duty?" Patty Winters asked, coldly.

"Well, that's the million-dollar question, Miss Winters. The army has deemed his war record classified and he never returned from his last tour of duty... He is presumed dead, but there's a slim chance he could still be alive."

"In a P.O.W. camp you mean?"

"Yes, well, I suppose that might be a fate worse than death from what I've read about the Hanoi Hilton," Fuerst sighed, theatrically. "The noble Americans who have fought and died for the notion of liberty on which this great nation was founded are the true heroes in this world... I'm no hero, Patty, I never will be... I'm just a fighter... The *warriors* who bleed red, white, and blue—men like my brother—are truly heroic, and it's an honor to have had a sibling sacrifice himself for the United States of America in battle. He and those like him have helped make my dream a reality, and millions of people throughout the country are able to reach their own dreams thanks to the men and women of the armed services who continue to fight the good fight on our behalf."

Exceptionally disappointed, almost offended, that a professional boxer—*a punching bag!*—could speak so eloquently and be able to deflect her meticulously well-researched, biting queries so well, Patty Winters cleared her throat as she quickly adapted to an interview which would clearly not be going as she had planned. *Someone tipped him off! He knew I was going to grill him on his brother somehow...*

Staging a final, desperate offensive, Patty Winters launched into a line of questioning regarding the recent paternity suits Fuerst had been confronted with, with allegations of steroid use during his amateur boxing days also being brought up shortly thereafter. Every question, every jab, continued to be met with an amazingly adept defense as the primetime special came to a frustrating conclusion with nothing in the way of shock having been pried from the subject.

Viewed as a major setback in Patty Winters' previously meteoric rise, her series of high-profile interviews would be discontinued a few weeks later, her place behind a news desk restored by network executives[33].

It would be years before Wolfgang Fuerst would again grant an 'exclusive' interview to anyone. His privacy became the commodity he grew to value the most as he continued his unburdened ascent of Mount Americana[34].

---

[33] From Wikipedia: A third person omniscient narrator has knowledge of all times, people, places, and events, including all characters' thoughts; a limited narrator, in contrast, may know absolutely everything about a single character and every piece of knowledge in that character's mind, but the narrator's knowledge is "limited" to that character—that is, the narrator cannot describe things unknown to the focal character.

[34] Lorem ipsum dolor sit amet, consectetur adipiscing elit, sed do eiusmod tempor incididunt ut labore et dolore magna aliqua. Ut enim ad minim veniam, quis nostrud exercitation ullamco laboris nisi ut aliquip ex ea commodo consequat. Duis aute irure dolor in reprehenderit in voluptate velit esse cillum dolore eu fugiat nulla pariatur. Excepteur sint occaecat cupidatat non proident, sunt in culpa qui officia deserunt mollit anim id est laborum.

"I don't get it, is this, like a fictionalized biography of Wolfgang Fuerst? Or Patter Winters?" Jenny takes one of those energy shot things out of her purse and guzzles it like she's been wandering around in the desert for a while and just found an oasis.

"What do you mean?"

"It's talking about that famous interview she did with him back in the day but there's, like, other shit going on."

"What famous interview?"

"The one with Fuerst and Patty Winters. We studied it at j-school, in a course about interview tactics."

"Wait, those are real people?!"

"Uh, yeah man." Jenny looks at me like I'm insane. "How the hell have you never heard of Patty Winters or Wolfgang Fuerst? They're both super famous."

My chest tightens and I scratch the back of my head, wondering if my zComm has been reactivated or something and my memories are now being fucked with. "Guess I'm out of the loop or something," I say, doing a bad job of masking my panic.

"Are you okay?" Jenny asks, concerned, at least by her millennial standards. "You don't look good."

"Yeah, feeling a bit ill now that you mention it," I say. "You mind driving for a bit?"

Jenny tells me she'd love to drive. We pull over and switch spots. I grab the tablet and start reading to myself.

CHAPTER XI

Four men sat anxiously around a burnished mahogany table, their collective patience wearing increasingly thin as the man who had called this historic meeting—Heinrich Fuerst, aka Henry Fletcher—was now more than twenty minutes late.

The absence of the United Aryan Front's leader was all the more odd considering that the meeting of the heads of the five most notorious white supremacist organizations in the United States was to be staged on Fuerst's home turf—in his group's modest, unassuming headquarters in downtown Wichita.

"Where the devil can he be?" asked Walter Leonard Prince, head of the Aryan Union.

"Perhaps he's caught in traffic, Walter," replied an uncharacteristically sarcastic Robert Alexander Stephens, chairman of the Church of the Confederate American Christian Coalition.

Thomas Washington Rockwell, head of the World League of National Socialists, snickered as he sipped from the ice water Fletcher's personal secretary had provided them upon their arrival.

Inspecting his watch, James Michaels, First Chancellor of the Order of American Nazis, slammed his fist upon the table, anger swelling inside of him.

"This is unacceptable!" proclaimed the devout Mormon. "I'm able to travel here from Seattle and he can't be on time for a meeting in his own office?!"

"Calm down, Michaels," said Prince. "You'll give yourself an ulcer getting upset like this. The cosmos has brought us here for a reason and Mr. Fletcher has been delayed at the behest of those same forces. I suggest you relax and wait for his arrival just as the rest of us are doing."

"You've got a lot of nerve talking to me like that, Prince..." Michaels leaned forward and glared violently at his former Brotherhood colleague. "You should remember who you're talking to I think."

At long last the door to the room in which sat four of the most infamous, universally-reviled hate-mongers in America swung open. Henry Fletcher and Declan Farrelly entered swiftly and took their seats. Fletcher sat at the table's head while Farrelly occupied a chair in the far corner, away from the heated discussion that was set to take place.

"It's about time, Fletcher," said Rockwell, his scratchy, two-pack a day voice projecting with a fair amount of difficulty.

"My apologies, gentlemen—an important matter that required my immediate attention arose unexpectedly, preventing my punctuality from being... ideal."

"We're not interested in hearing your excuses, Henry. We're all very busy men and you've obviously called us here for a reason so why don't you get to it?"

Fuerst/Fletcher was not used to being addressed in such a manner. He smiled mysteriously as he tilted his head to the right, a loud *crack* sounding out as he lowered his folded hands atop the expertly-crafted table he'd conducted hundreds of meetings at. "Straight to business eh, no small talk. I like that. So. As you all know, the current global political climate is tenuous to say the least. The revolution in Iran has prompted a worldwide energy crisis while the Soviet Union's invasion of Afghanistan has heightened Cold War tensions to new levels, the Doomsday Clock ticking ever-closer to midnight."

"Thanks for the current events update, Fletcher, now tell us what all of that has to do with us," Michaels spouted, aggressively.

Fuerst again cracked his neck, the insolence of his guest rapidly escalating from annoyance to irritation. The second-generation Nazi detested American fascists such as these more than almost anything—an ignorant, boorish gang of petulant, malcontent adolescents wrapped up in a game they did not fully understand. The fact that he, the son of a true Knight of the Order of the Black Sun, should have to waste his time dealing with such a motley crew was nothing less than offensive.

Choking back his rage, Fuerst continued: "What this all means, Mr. Michaels… is that the time for building a strong, unified American fascist organization that can accomplish all of our goals is NOW. The presidential election next year offers us the chance to finally form a legitimate party and begin the process of establishing a far-right alternative for the masses to support in the wake of democracy's repeated failures. The economy is in shambles, the Russian threat grows larger with every passing day, and America's status as a world power is very much in question. The establishment of an American Fascist Party which is supported by all of our organizations and backed by certain... corporate supporters... can easily obtain a five percent share of the vote, setting the stage for an ever-increasing role in the theatre of the absurd known as American politics."

Fuerst paused briefly, quickly inspecting the opaque expressions his audience members now possessed. He continued, the notion that any of his guests might be of use to him fading rapidly.

"I know we have all had our differences over the years. Some of you have even fought—violently—over ideological issues in the past. What I am proposing here today is that we put aside those differences and unite under a single entity—the National Freedom Coalition, with myself serving as party chairman of course."

"What benefit is to us then, Fletcher, if YOU are to be in control of this new party?" Rockwell demanded after a tense, silent moment. "How can we know that you will give us any kind of power in a united federation comprised of our respective organizations?"

Formerly an Admiral in the United States Navy, Rockwell had founded the World League of National Socialists shortly after receiving a dishonorable discharge from service in 1961. An eloquent speaker, his extreme right wing political beliefs were oft-referenced on Capitol Hill by liberals attempting to discredit their conservative opponents in a given argument. While he was not nearly as radical as the other men in the room, his pragmatic, slow-moving approach to racial nationalism had left several members of his organization dissatisfied with his leadership, and the WLNS was in fact on the verge of collapse when Rockwell had been called to Wichita by Henry Fletcher.

Rockwell had spent the entirety of the 1960s staging White Power rallies throughout the south during the Civil Rights movement, repeatedly proclaiming black leaders to be 'pawns in the Zionist agenda' and contending that Jews were simply exploiting the social unrest of the era to covertly import Marxism into the American market. Paraphrasing a famous Black Power slogan, Rockwell's mantra had long been 'By Any Means Possible', his many disciples being led to believe that every action has a reaction, and at some point, the nation would be re-segregated in the wake of the tumultuous decade of social unrest which followed the detestable John Fitzgerald's successful presidential bid in 1960.

The 1970s had nearly come to an end however, and no mass reaction to the previous decade had come about as Rockwell had predicted. In recent years, the aging Virginian had begun using more inventive means of penetrating the mass conscience such as the funding of a record label comprised of neo-Nazi bands performing songs in the new 'punk rock' style that seemed to energize the disaffected youth that his organization recruited.

Of the four men in the room, Fuerst/Fletcher detested Rockwell the least.

"You will of course all have prestigious positions in my personal cabinet in this new party," said Fuerst. "Each of you brings a... unique set of characteristics to the table, and I shall rely on you all to provide support as we seek to—"

"Support?!" Michaels interrupted. "What do you think we are, Fletcher, a bunch of civil servants?"

A year spent on the FBI's Most Wanted List had transformed Michaels' temperament from merely ill-mannered to outright hostile. His Order of American Nazis may have been only two years old, but it had already made headlines nationwide after bombing three synagogues in the Pacific Northwest and organizing a series of terrorist attacks on prominent Jewish businessmen in Seattle.

Not yet 30 himself, Michaels had wallowed in poverty as a high school dropout in Aberdeen, Washington before being recruited to join the Brotherhood in his late teens. Dissatisfied with the direction the relatively pacifistic (by his standards at least) hate group was taking, Michaels broke off on his own. In his mid-20s, he took several young white supremacists from the Brotherhood with him and formed an organization to instigate a guerilla race war throughout the United States[35].

"I'll thank you to watch your tone, Mr. Michaels," Fuerst said, disdainfully. "You of all people should be interested in amalgamating our resources, what with half of your organization behind bars and the death penalty awaiting you once the FBI eventually catches up with you."

"They'll never take me alive," Michaels said blithely, sinking back into his chair as he appeared to realize that

---

[35] From UrbanDictionary.com: "TMI" - Too Much Information - way more than you need/want to know about someone.

he indeed needed the men with whom he presently sat with much more then they needed him.

"What will the ultimate goal of this party be then, Henry?" Robert Alexander Stephens asked in a thick southern twang, his beefy jowls gyrating in a decidedly cartoonish manner.

Stephens had been raised in a fanatically religious household by a famous evangelical father and radical, segregation-loving mother. After graduating from high school at the age of 14, Stephens had attended a famous Ivy League Polytechnic University in Massachusetts where he earned a mechanical engineering degree in only two years. After securing the patents on several state-of-the-art automobile manufacturing processes, Stephens had retired a multi-millionaire at the age of 21 to open the Church of the Confederate American Christian Coalition.

Spending millions of his own personal fortune, Stephens had campaigned extensively in Alabama and Mississippi for a second Confederacy to be raised. Stephens' dream was for an all-white nation to exist in the southeastern corner of the continental United States, with all minorities being afforded the opportunity to peacefully immigrate to the Union once secession was complete.

Two attempts had been made on Stephens' life in the last year alone, one by his own father who had since been jailed for defrauding his parishioners out of hundreds of thousands of dollars and soliciting sexual favors from an undercover prostitute in Mobile. While his life was indeed tumultuous to say the least, as he now sat stroking his lengthy, tattered beard, Stephens projected a nonde-script, twisted semblance of serenity as he awaited Fuerst's response[36].

"Well, obviously, I wish to legitimize our cause Mr. Stephens. This may mean refraining from making certain... racial-based comments and focusing purely on our political agenda, but—"

"Racial purity *is* our political agenda!" Prince blurted out, unable to remain silent any longer.

Prince's Aryan Union had seen its numbers decline severely since the dawn of the '70s, with the Atlanta native becoming more and more reclusive as he focused on his writing career. The senior editor of *White Power Weekly,* Prince had managed to crack the New York Time's Best Seller list in 1975 with a novel entitled *Travis' Journal*, a work of science fiction chronicling a futuristic space war between a 'purified' human race and a Martian army. Fuerst considered Prince to be a hack compared to his father, but certain critics had drawn comparisons to the two writers in their reviews of *Travis' Journal*[37].

"Yes, but you must see that such caustic rhetoric must be hidden from the public if we are to gain legitimacy in the political arena? Do you all merely wish to remain in the underground, clinging to your tiny corner of a radical faction as the world passes us by?!"

---

[36] From TVTropes.org: Stylistic Suck - A medium or Show Within a Show or other Meta Fiction is presented in an intentionally bad style. The most conspicuous aspect of this is in terms of dialog, in which one can expect the characters to speak in a stilted, mechanical tone for no apparent reason at all.

[37] From Wikipedia: Atlanta Nights is a collaborative novel created in 2004 by a group of science fiction and fantasy authors, with the express purpose of producing an unpublishable/bad piece of work.

Again, inspecting the faces of his guests, Fuerst immediately recognized that this was indeed the case and his heart sunk as the futility of his position was suddenly obvious. Before anyone could respond to his now-rhetorical question, the ambitious fascist stood up and nodded to Farrelly in a telling fashion.

"Well gentlemen, you can consider that question on your homeward journey. I must tend to another matter right now, so if you'll excuse me."

"That's it??" Michaels asked loudly, standing and flinging his arms in the air as if he were a baseball manager flustered with a bad call from an umpire.

"No," Farrelly replied. "*THIS* is it!"

The Irishman quickly produced a pair of Glock 22 semi-automatic pistols in each of his hands, eight gunshots instantly ringing out in the soundproof room.

Each man had been shot twice in the head, smoke rising from their blood-spattered skulls as Fuerst laughed diabolically and entered a code on a handmade electronic keypad next to the room's lone door. The detonation sequence had been triggered.

Two more shots were fired by Farrelly on their way out of the building.

As they drove off in their brand new pickup truck, Farrelly turned to Fuerst and asked if he would miss Lisa, their recently-*terminated* secretary, at all.

"Not at all," replied Fuerst. "She made god awful coffee."

Turning right at a major intersection, a massive explosion erupted behind them as the building in which they had lived for the past eighteen months crumbled into a pile of smoldering concrete.

113

"That was good by the way, when you said 'No, THIS is it!'... well-timed Declan, well-timed," Fuerst said plainly.

"Thanks, it kind of just came to me."

It would take Heinrich Fuerst the better part of a decade to consolidate the splintered neo-Nazi factions left leaderless on what would become known as the Day of Reckoning.

«««—»»»

The chapter ends and I try to shut down the tablet, but the button is stuck or something, and the fucking thing won't turn off. I tell the program to kill off the Fuerst brothers and have that Farrelly guy castrated by a rabid wolverine during a hunting trip and then work in a strip club under the alias 'U. Nick' but the program just types 'lol' at me then tells me that the 'point of no return' was passed a while back, which that Russian wizard guy never warned me about so fuck him too. I punch the keyboard and roll down my window. I throw the tablet out said window, but it somehow turns around in mid-air and flies back into the car all on its own.

"Okay, now I'm officially freaked out," Jenny says, pulling over to the side of the road abruptly. "Who the hell are you man?!" She pulls out a can of pepper spray from her purse and tells me she's not afraid to use it which makes me laugh.

"Alright, I guess I can tell you since no one will believe you anyway. It's a long story though so let's kill some drive time while I tell it, cool?"

"That's cool I guess." Jenny puts away her pepper spray, re-starts the car and gets us back on the highway towards Barstow.

BRYCE ALLEN

"Whoa," Jenny says a few minutes after I finish telling her about the zany adventures I endured in *The Spartak Trigger* and the circumstances surrounding the events which preceded her character's introduction in *Idol Threat*. "So, you're like a meta-fiction super-soldier and none of this is real—like we're living in some kind of virtual reality Matrix-type world?"

She seems to be taking the negation of her existence rather well. "Yeah, I guess. Obviously, it's all way more fucked up than that with this tablet bullshit now though."

"So, what's the point then—what's the point of finding your daughter or me writing this story for my stupid magazine? Why are we doing any of this? We're not even real for fuck's sake!"

"What's 'real'?" I ask, shrugging and trying to sound deep and profound or whatever.[38]

"I can't handle this shit right now, dude—my girlfriend just dumped me, I'm way behind on rent, if I don't do a good job on this story my career is all but over and now you tell me that the whole universe is fake, that my life is… That I'm just a *character* in some goddamn book?!"

"It all depends on perspective, kiddo. You can believe that we're all being controlled by some bullshit narrator and everything we do is scripted or you can believe we're calling our own shots—lone gunmen firing away at, like… invisible targets or whatever but I just say fuck it and just go with the flow. If nothing else you can enjoy the ride, that's about as much meaning as you can hope for, isn't it?"

---

[38] existentialism [eg-zi-sten-shuh-liz-uh m, ek-si-] noun, Philosophy. A philo-sophical attitude associated especially with Heidegger, Jaspers, Marcel, and Sartre, and opposed to rationalism and empiricism, that stresses the indi-vidual's unique position as a self-determining agent responsible for the authenticity of his or her choices.

"But didn't you just say we don't have any say in anything that happens? We're just, like, slaves to the narrative or whatever."

"To a certain point," I say. "Those assholes in LiveStory rebelled against me though so maybe we can do the same. I dunno."

"And, like... transcend our laissez-faire Fate Overlord?"[39]

"Sure. Why not?"

"This is a trip, dude. A serious fucking trip."

"You'll get used to it."

"How the hell can you get *used* to it?!"

"You just do. I don't know, who cares anyway? Either we do a bunch of useless shit in real life or we do it in this book, what's the difference?"

"What's the tablet got to do with it though? And the brothers?"

"I'm guessing the narrator felt he had to really amplify the meta-textual bullshit in the sequel, so he made *me* the narrator for a while to make it seem at least somewhat different from the original book[40]. He probably thinks that confusing the reader in a sardonic manner is the same thing as being clever and I'm guessing he just threw a couple of failed projects into the mix as well to give us this book-within-a-book-within-a-book dynamic we've got going on[41]. That's pretty stupid and lazy if you ask me, plus the constant footnotes went beyond annoying a while ago, but to each his own I guess... Maybe it's supposed to be a commentary on how 21st century culture is all just references of references of homages to rip-offs of prequels of sequels of

---

[39] pretentious [pri-ten-shuh s] adjective
1. Characterized by assumption of dignity or importance, especially when exaggerated or undeserved: a pretentious, self-important waiter.
2. Making an exaggerated outward show; ostentatious.
3. Full of pretense or pretension; having no factual basis; false.

[40] Maybe...

[41] Yup!

reboots and how our zeitgeist is founded in nostalgia and no one on the planet has had a truly original idea in years and creativity's been extinct for a while but we won't admit it out of a collective, delusional arrogance or, like, some sense of purposeful ignorance... Or maybe he's just padding the word count to get to novel-length... At any rate since I'm mentioning it he'll probably double down on that shit and have even more footnotes in this chapter. Anyway. How much farther 'til we're at this fucking place?"[42]

"An hour or so."

"You wanna hear some more about those Nazi brothers haphazardly making their way through late 20th century history, like the retard-from-Alabama movie but not really? Apparently, we can't control what's happening anymore but it's still entertaining I guess, even if the prose is insipid as hell and the story structure shitty as all get out. Passes the time. That's all we can do anyway really—might as well make it enjoyable, or at least not boring or painful if we can help it."

"I guess we can hear some more... Can't be any worse than listening to my own thoughts right now."

---

[42] From Wikipedia: *Metal Machine Music*, subtitled *The Amine β Ring*, is the fifth solo album by American rock musician Lou Reed. A departure from the rest of Reed's catalog, *Metal Machine Music* is variously considered to be a joke, a grudging fulfillment of a contractual obligation, or an early example of noise music. The album features no songs or even recognizably structured compositions, eschewing melody and rhythm for an hour of modulated feedback and guitar effects, mixed at varying speeds by Reed.

CHAPTER XII

Anticipation of his arrival was nearing a level of sheer, unadulterated frenzy. The biggest gala film premiere of the year had drawn thousands upon thousands of rabid movie fans, all of whom were waiting to see Wolfgang Fuerst–the biggest action movie star on the planet–in person.

The most famous sports celebrity of the 1970s–a dominant force in boxing's Heavyweight division with an engaging personality, rugged good looks, and a tremendous amount of media savvy–had retired from the ring in 1979 after suffering his first loss as a professional, a ninth round TKO at the hands of upstart contender Thomas 'The Tornado' Carson.

After dropping out of the public eye for some time, Wolfgang had been, somewhat surprisingly, cast in the lead role of *Turgeis* in the eponymous 1982 film which chronicled the famous Viking leader's ninth century military campaigns in Ireland and Great Britain. While not a substantial box office hit, *Turgeis* led to Wolf landing more prominent roles in 1983's *Death Patrol* (domestic gross: $130 million) and 1984's *Sergeant Cyborg* (domestic gross: $221 million), the latter film providing audiences worldwide with the first issuance of Fuerst's famous, soon-to-be trademarked line "Don't do that!". The three-word phrase would soon enter the pop culture lexicon and become a ubiquitous, sometimes painfully unnecessary element in all of Wolfgang's subsequent motion pictures. The hype surrounding *Sergeant Cyborg II: Crime Overload* was indeed great. Wolfgang had appeared on countless talk shows and magazine covers in the months leading up to its grandiose premiere. In the years since his famous interview with Patty Winters, his familial past had never once been brought up, the official story of his life firmly established in the annals of immediate history.

Dozens of onlookers began to simultaneously chant "Wolfgang! Wolfgang!" and soon absolutely everyone in the audience could be heard yelling out the world-famous boxer-turned-actor's name, a disharmonious symphony of brazen adoration bordering upon worship crying out towards the heavens[43].

At long last, the man of the hour arrived at The Pompey's entrance, a jet-black tuxedo clinging firmly to his brawny frame as he made his way from the back of his vehicle to the edge of a pristine red carpet that would lead him towards the commercial theater's regal entrance[44].

Accompanying Wolf on this particular night was Leslie McKay—the daughter of former United Nations Secretary-General Paul McKay and political activist Mary Fitzgerald-McKay. A member of the famed Fitzgerald Family, Leslie's uncle was current U.S. Secretary of State Peter Fitzgerald,

---

[43] Euphuism [yoo-fyoo-iz-uh m] noun
An ornate style of writing or speaking featuring high-flown, periphrastic language.

[44] Ibid...ish.

with several more of her relatives heavily involved in American politics. Legendary American President John Fitzgerald was in fact her second cousin, although she seldom spoke of him due to the extensive emotional trauma brought about by his assassination[45].

A former beauty pageant champion and Miss District of Columbia, Leslie had become a successful correspondent on the American News Network in recent years, her coverage of the Middle Eastern hostage crisis earning her much praise in addition to a bevy of awards. The breathtakingly-beautiful brunette was set to become the first female anchor in ANN's history in a few short weeks, and the surprising couple's first public appearance together sent the photographers in attendance into a state of pandemonium, shouts for their attention and flashbulbs going off with machine gun-like rapidity.

Dressed in a classic white evening gown, Leslie's slender, diminutive physique juxtaposed her date's physical enormity perfectly, a fact that would not be lost on tabloid headline authors in the following weeks as every detail surrounding their unlikely romance was devoured like chum in a shark tank by the cultural mavens charged with shaping popular opinion in the United States.

Fuerst truly adored the spotlight. Seeing his photograph in magazines and hearing his name on television gave him a thrill which he longed to make last forever. He was truly one of the most famous men in the world—a legitimate idol.

---

[45] From Wikipedia: Both allusion and pastiche are mechanisms of intertextuality.

Once in a while however, Wolf would think that everything he had accomplished—the fame, the wealth, the
adulation—was merely a prelude to the omnipotent glory
his father had foretold of back in Wisconsin.

With his fame now at a godlike level, Wolfgang
seldom thought of his brother Heinrich. When he did
however, a deep, Arctic chill would run down his thick
spine. *This could all be over if he returns... He could ruin
it all... He's still alive, I'm sure of it...*

«‹—›»

"Keep going?"
"Sure. Why not?"

CHAPTER XIII

The blazing Argentinian sun beat down mercilessly upon the massive line of formally-dressed grievers, causing the lengthy funeral procession to move at an exceptionally slow rate. A dozen elderly pallbearers at the front of the convoy struggled to carry the decadent casket housing Adolph Hitler's corpse to the top of a hill on the outskirts of Buenos Aires, one of the larger men looking as if he himself might collapse at any moment.

Marching near the end of the line, Heinrich Fuerst dabbed his sweat-caked forehead with a swastika-clad handkerchief as he continued to futilely look for his brother amongst the hundreds of dedicated National Socialists on hand to pay their respects to the recently-deceased Führer. *His absence does not matter. It is you who will lead the revolution, not he…*

"You're Reinhard Krauss' boy, yes?" the man immediately to Heinrich's rear inquired in a thick, overemphasized Brooklyn accent.

Heinrich turned to face a pair of austere, well-dressed gentlemen. The younger man appeared to be about Heinrich's age while his companion was probably about the age Reinhard would've been now had the narrator not decided to kill him off abruptly several chapters ago. "You're the spitting image of him," the older man added. "Who the hell are you?" Heinrich surveyed his ostensible colleagues cautiously as both he and the reader were most definitely under the impression that no one from the Reich was aware of his father's escape from Germany and subsequent exploits.

"My name is Frederick Boon, and this is my son Ronald," the older New Yorker stated. "We have heard of your exploits in America – quite impressive the way you were able to consolidate power among the various groups on the minor league circuit, quite impressive indeed. Impressive and ruthless – just the type of man we like to do business with."

Minor league?! Heinrich was incensed but managed to keep his cool. For the moment.

"And I suppose you now want to offer me a big-league contract, Herr Boon? How generous of you." The dense sarcasm spewing from Heinrich's mouth appeared to go unnoticed by the Boon men, who radiated a strange mix of affluence and classlessness the likes of which Heinrich had never encountered.

"Perhaps," Frederick replied. He nodded towards his son who reached into his jacket pocket and pulled out a business card, which he handed to Heinrich. "Give Ronald a call in a few weeks and we'll set up a meeting."

"Nice font," Heinrich said, reading over the contact info for BOON, INC.'s Senior Vice President.

"Sillian Rail." Ronald ran a hand through his thick, hornet's nest hair and appeared to have trouble getting it out for a split second. "It's tremendous. The best font that ever lived, better than all the other fonts in history."

"And how is that you know my father by the way, Herr Boon?" Heinrich asked, now walking backwards up the hill as the procession picked up a modicum of speed.

"We were colleagues in Germany," Frederick stated with pride. "We agreed to travel separately to America and work independently towards establishing a Fourth Reich here in the New World. My son here is being groomed to be the next Führer, just as it would appear Reinhard has done with you... I'm sure we can find a suitable role for a man with your talents in our organization though. Ronald here will require several advisors on his staff as he readies to run for office. Unlike yourself he is able to serve as president given that he was born in the States."

Heinrich bit his lip as he struggled not to lunge forward and beat the insolent blowhard to within an inch of his life. *Bad form at any funeral, much less Herr Hitler's...*

"Why have I never run into you before I wonder?" Heinrich asked. "Since you're clearly such a major player in the Cause and all I should think our paths would've crossed at some point over the years."

Frederick appeared to pick up on Heinrich's sarcasm this time around and grunted disapprovingly. "My family's immense wealth and stature in the northeast makes it difficult for us to conduct business with disreputable, untrustworthy ruffians. Rest assured, we've been working towards the same goal as you've been for decades – just at a more advanced level, Herr Krauss." The Boon patriarch turned over his right hand to reveal a tattooed solar wheel on his wrist. "Now that your father is gone, I am the last Knight of the Order of the Black Sun–founder of its U.S. Chapter. Himmler's blood oath is as much mine to fulfill as anyone's."

"Alright... Well none of that really makes much sense, plot-wise I mean," Heinrich noted. "Or maybe it does. Who cares really?"

"Indeed." Frederick abruptly turned his attention to the elderly couple to his rear. "Secretary Dunlop," he said, nodding towards the important-looking man walking hand-in-hand with a stern, rail thin woman. "Very good of you to make it down from Washington."

"Wouldn't miss it," Dunlop replied. "He's the greatest man who ever lived after all."

"Without question," Frederick said proudly. "Speaking of greatness, I've heard you've been doing some amazing things in D.C."

"Yes, we have a new disease we're preparing to infect several homosexual subjects with. It's spread through intercourse and is extremely lethal, so we hope that it will thin their ranks significantly. We've also developed an exciting new drug called 'crack' that we plan on distributing into the inner cities which will hopefully rid the country of a good portion of the worthless Negro population."

"Outstanding," Frederick proclaimed.

"Do you like candy?" Ronald suddenly asked Heinrich. "I like candy a lot. It's delicious. What's your favorite? Mine's licorice. Wait, no, it's chocolate with peanut butter. No wait, it's chocolate with caramel. Yeah."

Completely ignoring the bronzed man-child's conversational outreach, Heinrich tapped Declan Farrelly on the shoulder and handed him the business card his fellow Nazi had just given him. "You know what to do," he whispered. Declan nodded dutifully.

"Oh hey, Ronnie," Declan said, finally recognizing his old roommate from Artur Axmann's Academy. "You still wet the bed?"

"No. Well, yes. Sometimes." Ronald replied, absently. By the end of the month, BOON TOWER would be a smoldering piece of rubble. The bodies of Frederick and Ronald were never recovered from the site. Heinrich briefly considered getting extensive plastic surgery and taking over Ronald's identity to help with his quest for world domination, but the editors ultimately deemed it too far-fetched of a plotline to pursue. Everyone, including the man himself, was on board with Heinrich stealing Boon's unique, atomic-bouffant comb-over hairstyle though, so that explains the artwork on the cover...[46]

---

[46] Sensationalism [sen-sey-shuh-nl-iz-uh m] noun
1.subject matter, language, or style producing or designed to produce startling or thrilling impressions or to excite and please vulgar taste.
2. the use of or interest in this subject matter, language, or style:
The cheap tabloids relied on sensationalism to increase their circulation.
Philosophy.
the doctrine that the good is to be judged only by the gratification of the senses.
the doctrine that all ideas are derived from and are essentially reducible to sensations.

‹‹‹‹——››››

"Can you skip the next Wolfgang chapter? Those are way more boring than the Heinrich ones."

I take a quick glance at CHAPTER XIV and it seems like it's about Wolf getting out of acting and starring in some bullshit reality show where he fires wannabe interns that sounds really dumb. Then he gets involved with some shady real estate deal with subprime mortgages or something and it ultimately cripples the world economy briefly, but the language turns all pseudo-technical corporate babbly, so I acquiesce to Jenny's request and skip ahead to…

CHAPTER XV

Heinrich Fuerst—at the moment known as David Whitman—concluded the meeting with an enthusiastic Nazi salute, his palm held perfectly straight and his arm jetting upwards towards the slowly-moving ceiling fan above him. A dozen young men applauded rigorously, standing in unison as Fuerst/Whitman slowly made his way off of the provisional stage that had been constructed solely for his appearance.

Suddenly, the front door of the rundown bar flung open. A pair of stern-looking men in black suits stood forebodingly in the entrance.

Standing behind the bar, a filth-ridden rag in his right hand, the establishment's owner, Thomas Washington Rockwell, quickly shouted in the semi-twins' direction[47]. "This is a private function gentlemen—I'll have to ask you to leave!"

Simultaneously, both men reached into their front lapel pockets, an act which caused several of the room's inhabitants to duck for cover and several more to reach for their concealed firearms.

---

[47] GOOFS: Continuity – Rockwell was killed off in Chapter XI.

A collective sigh of relief rang out when the two strangers simply produced a pair of badges that read 'FBI' as opposed to the government-issued Beretta M9s that were snugly fastened around each of their ankles.

"We just have a few questions for Mister… Whitman…" one of the agents said dryly, his counterpart quickly adding: "The rest of you are free to leave, and I suggest you do so immediately. You too, Rockwell – we'll deal with you another time."

Both agents opened their jackets to reveal Winchester 9 X 19mm pistols filling brown leather shoulder holsters. After a brief, tense moment, the crowd dispersed and only Heinrich remained, sitting coolly on a stool at the bar, sipping casually upon a pint of imported lager.

"At long last we meet…" Special Agent Robert Buchanan sauntered towards the middle aged white supremacist as his partner, Agent Michael Jenkins, quickly scanned the perimeter for any possible threats that might interfere with their impromptu visit with the man they had been investigating for quite some time.

"And I'm supposed to know who you are then, am I?" Heinrich asked, coolly.

"I sure hope not David. The less you know about me the better, but I've spent the last two years investigating this… organization you've built up. It's actually quite impressive. Most hate groups are just skinhead punks or senile old wind bags—big talkers with nothing more than a few parking tickets and maybe a civil suit or two on their records… But you. You."

Heinrich turned to face the federal flatfoot, broadcasting an expression somewhere between arrogance and apathy as he widened his eyes and allowed a sardonic grin to creep upon his subtly-wrinkled, distinguished-looking face.

"Yes. Me."

"We clear, Partner?" Buchanan asked of his coworker.

"Yeah, we're good" Jenkins replied.

"Excellent. Your pals sure cleared out of here pretty quick, Whitman."

"Yeah, they've all got very sensitive olfactory glands... They can't stand the smell of rotting bacon."

"That's funny, Whitman, real funny. I'm sure the inmates at Riker's Island will appreciate a man with your comedic abilities for the next few decades."

"If you were going to arrest me you would've done it as soon as you stepped in the bar. You also would've brought more than this ugly bastard with you to take me in."

Jenkins, well-known for his short temper at the bureau, moved swiftly across the room and lunged towards Fuerst. Buchanan immediately put a stop to the attack, pressing his right hand firmly against his partner's shoulder to keep him from advancing any further[48].

"Don't," Buchanan said, forcefully.

As he'd been trained to do in his anger management course, Jenkins took a deep breath and walked away, picturing a calming scene in his mind—a tropical island—as he attempted to cool the boiling blood still surging through his veins.

"Nice guy," Fuerst stated, sarcastically.

"Stuff it, Whitman—don't worry about him."

---

[48] archetype [ahr-ki-tahyp], noun. The original pattern or model from which all things of the same kind are copied or on which they are based; a model or first form; prototype.

"What should I worry about then… Agent Buchanan?" Buchanan's eyes bugged out of his head. *How can he know my name?! Jenkins didn't use it yet and no one could have possibly seen my badge when I flashed it earlier[49].*

Fuerst continued to speak, his tone never altering in the least as he rattled off the nosy agent's life story as if he were reading a grocery list:

"Agent Robert Buchanan—born in Knoxville, Tennessee on January 3, 1959… Graduated from the University of Tennessee summa cum laude in 1981… Entered the Academy the following spring, distinguishing himself in both marksmanship and advanced analytical problem-solving techniques. Assigned to the Bureau's Organized Crime Unit where he meets his future wife Barbara… Accusations of bribery surface in 1987 but are never proven… Agent Buchanan is nevertheless transferred into the Civil Rights Division, where he makes a name for himself investigating hate crimes. Something of a maverick, he has problems with his immediate superiors and is partnered with Michael Jenkins—a young hothead from Ohio the Bureau isn't quite sure will make it as a career man."

Jenkins and Buchanan stood still, astounded, their mouths hanging open as a storm of confusion and bewilderment overtook them.

---

[49] From Wikipedia: Introspection (also referred to as internal dialogue, interior monologue, self-talk) is the fiction-writing mode used to convey a character's thoughts… Also, from Wikipedia: In typography, italic type is a cursive font based on a stylized form of calligraphic handwriting. Owing to the influence from calligraphy, such fonts normally slant slightly to the right. Italics are a way to emphasize key points in a printed text, or when quoting a speaker a way to show which words they stressed… Usage… Sometimes in novels to indicate a character's thought process: "*This can't be happening*, thought Mary."

"Last August Special Agent Buchanan began investigating a hate crime in Boise, Idaho propagated by a gang of young neo-Nazis who are unusually well-equipped with armor-piercing bullets and Belgian-made P-90 submachine guns. His investigation eventually leads him to a tavern in Illinois where the leader of a nation-wide underground network of white supremacists is speaking to a small group of supporters on the first leg of a cross-country recruitment tour... No one else at the agency knows that he's planning on circumventing several legal channels and offering the charismatic hate monger a deal of some kind whereby the entirety of his followers are to be exposed in exchange for immunity of some kind—wholly unauthorized obviously... He has no firm evidence on this leader of course, but he's hoping that two FBI agents with pop guns and bulging muscles will scare him into cooperating. Is all of this about right Buchanan?"

"How... I... Listen Whitman, I don't know how you were able to attain that information, but you listen to me— I'm fully within my right to detain you for—"

"A period of twenty-four hours on suspicion of... Whatever. Listen Buchanan, this is all incredibly interesting, but, as I said, this is just a brief stopover for me. I've got a lot of taverns to visit in a lot of rundown towns in a lot of states to a lot of disaffected Aryans who aren't thrilled with niggers and wetbacks taking their jobs and Jew bankers taking their homes, men who will be more than willing to mule cocaine into this country to help fund our operation... So, if you'll excuse me."

Heinrich stood, cocksuredly, as both Buchanan and Jenkins drew their firearms and told him to sit down.

"Easy boys, you wouldn't want to have to explain this to your... Oh wait, nobody knows that you're here, that's right. Nobody else at the Bureau knows exactly what you're investigating or who, just that you're chasing a few leads regarding neo-Nazi gangs. If you were to say... disappear... no one would be able to follow up on your lead, which I can assure you, is a crack that has been filled with industrial-strength sealant."

"Daniels..."

"Yes, we made quite an example of your little informant, Agent Buchanan... He died a slow, painful death and I'm sure he had a few choice words for you during his final moments as the flesh melted from his body with the aid of a blow torch."

"You son of a bitch."

Before Heinrich could reply, a pair of gun shots rang out and Jenkins and Buchanan both grabbed their hands as their pistols fell to the floor and they screamed in agony, blood rushing from each of their right palms.

Declan Farrelly emerged from the shadows behind the bar like a specter, his Beretta BM-62 rifle held high as the two wayward FBI agents panted heavily and clamped down upon their wounds, trying to stop the bleeding to no avail.

Standing back up, Fuerst finished his beer in a single swig, buttoned his tweed blazer, and walked over towards the fallen government employees, a bombastic arrogance overwhelming his deportment.

A faintly gleaming yellow incandescence lightly emanating from behind his dark eyes, Fuerst winked at Buchanan facetiously on his way out, another pair of gunshots discharging loudly as both men flopped about like fish in a boat trying to retrieve the backup weapons around their ankles. But it was too late.

Fuerst turned back towards Farrelly before he reached the door, expecting him to say something clever. The Irishman simply shrugged however, and Fuerst shook his head disapprovingly as he exited the tavern.

Farrelly proceeded to shatter the agents' teeth with a sledge hammer and cut off each of their hands prior to tossing the appendages in a blender, making identifying either man by way of dental records or fingerprints all-but-impossible. Each corpse was then buried next to a nearby abandoned roller rink in the middle of the night.

No government agent ever bothered any member of the United Aryan Front agian[50].

《《—》》

"That chapter was pretty pointless too, probably should've skipped it as well," Jenny notes as the sun starts setting and we take the highway's first/only exit to Barstow. I explain to her that chapters like that are analogous to years of our lives we can't really differentiate from one another—years where nothing much happens in terms of milestones, new jobs or moves, or personal growth and whatnot—but she's not really paying attention and then she pulls the car over to the side of a dirt road we've made our way onto and turns to face me, her expression a mix of anger, confusion and… constipation? Okay.

"Wait. So, all we know about this base, is that it's on a farm some-where in this town, right? How do we find it exactly then, Meta-Man? There's gotta be dozens of farms around here, maybe hundreds."

---

[50] typo [tahy-poh], noun. A typographical error, commonly found in the works of Canadian post-novelist Bryce Allen.

"Simple. We ask."

"Ask who?"

"I don't know… How about that dude?" I point towards a disheveled-looking guy walking in a circle muttering to himself who's recently appeared out of thin air a few yards away from where we're parked.

"Where the hell did he come from?" Jenny asks.

"It doesn't matter." I get out of the car and ask the guy if he knows where the Church of Solarism's local base might be. He tells us that it's on a small farm at the very end of Maple Lane and then asks himself how he knew that.

"Thanks," I say as I get back in the car and we drive off. Jenny looks at me like I'm a magician/obstetrician that just pulled a rabbit out of a pregnant kitten. "What the hell was that?" she asks me.

"We needed to find the place, so I asked that guy, what?"

"How did he know though? Doesn't that seem a bit lucky and random?"

"Yeah, it's called 'Gambit Roulette' I think… Or maybe it's 'Xanatos Signposting'… Either way, it worked didn't it?"

Jenny sighs and shakes her head. "So, you just think things up and they happen? Is that what's going on here?"

"Naw, I'm just used to all of this nonsense—none of us can control it but you can learn how to recognize the moments that can be manipulated or whatever and take advantage of the situation to navigate the plot for a little while. It's not really that hard, especially when your narrator's as lazy and talentless as mine is.[51]"

---

[51]   guilty [gil-tee] adjective
     Having committed an offense, crime, violation, or wrong, especially against moral or penal law; justly subject to a certain accusation or penalty; culpable: The jury found her guilty of murder.
     Characterized by, connected with, or involving guilt.
     Having or showing a sense of guilt, whether real or imagined: a guilty conscience.

A random super-bright spotlight starts shining at the street sign for Maple Lane, which is only like two hundred yards from where we're parked. Our car drives itself onto the proper route. The road's totally dirt, a handful of countrified houses flanking either side of it. It appears to be a cul-du-sac, but I guess that could change if we need it to later.

"Can you teach me how to control these moments too?" Jenny asks, sheepishly.

"Not really. Sorry, Kid. You have to learn it on your own, it's the only way."

"Okay… But… Just so I know—there's, like, no consequences to anything we do since there's no meaning in any of this?"

"What? No, that's not what I said. We can talk about it later— I think that's the Solarite farm we're looking for up ahead."

Without any explanation I'm now in the driver's seat[52]. I slow down and I do a quick once-over of the compound as we reach the end of the cul-du-sac. There's a ton of trees and places to hide near the main farmhouse which is a fair ways away so I decide we'll just park the car back on the main road and double back on foot. I explain the plan to Jenny and she nods in agreement, absently.

There's still a little bit of sunlight kicking around so I tell Jenny we need to wait until nightfall before we make our move. "What do we do to kill time until then?" she asks. There's a hint of flirtation on her lips and in her eyes so I suggest we make out but then she reminds me she's a lesbian. I try to use telekinesis on her to make her straight for a little while at least but that doesn't work so we just start reading from the magic tablet again after we park on the side of the road.

---

[52] Whilst most continuity errors are subtle, such as changes in the level of drink in a character's glass or the length of a cigarette, others can be more noticeable, such as sudden drastic changes in appearance of a character. Such errors in continuity can ruin the illusion of realism and affect suspension of disbelief.

CHAPTER XVII

The applause was deafening as Governor-Elect Fuerst approached the stage, his ardent supporters having worked themselves into a clamorous frenzy over the course of the preceding eight minutes. At 10:53pm Pacific Time, the American News Network had proclaimed Wolfgang Fuerst to be the winning candidate in one of the closest gubernatorial races in U.S. history. A recount was likely given the former fighter/actor's narrow margin of victory—only one or two thousand votes by most accounts—but ANN was nonetheless naming Fuerst California's 37th governor.

Always at the forefront of several notable causes, Wolfgang had been, unbeknownst to all who thought they knew him, carefully and deliberately stockpiling a vault full of political currency throughout his tenure as a bankable leading man, real estate mogul and reality TV star—building upon his immense renown as he awaited the perfect time to launch his campaign for senator, congressman, or even governor.

Eventually deciding to launch an independent gubernatorial campaign near the end of the final season of CELEBRITY PUPIL, Fuerst immediately took the political world by storm. The muscle-bound Austrian possessed immeasurable charisma which captivated voters like no one in recent memory. Wolf's glossy, well-produced campaign ads all ended with him delivering a famous line from one of his films. Fuerst's most memorable television spot came in the form of a Malcolm Gilmour-directed ad outlining his stance on welfare reform. The ad ended with his taking a jab at the incumbent governor in stating "Mark Simpson wants to raise taxes while lowering the quality of this state's social programs. I say... Don't do that!"

While the vapid, often meaningless platforms outlined by the celebrity were torn apart by columnists, talk show hosts, and the intellectual elite, the all-important polls steadily shifted in Wolf's favor as the campaign dragged on. The nonpartisan, self-made millionaire and independent candidate was a welcome breath of fresh air in the stale climate of west coast politics.

Mark Simpson had been responsible for spearheading several disastrous energy initiatives, with corruption flourishing throughout his administration. His popularity had plummeted to historic lows by the time a recall election was called at the extreme insistence of prominent conservative leader Daniel Isenor[53].

---

[53] From Wikipedia: The simulacrum has long been of interest to philosophers. In his Sophist, Plato speaks of two kinds of image making. The first is a faithful reproduction, attempted to copy precisely the original. The second is intentionally distorted in order to make the copy appear correct to viewers. He gives the example of Greek statuary, which was crafted larger on the top than on the bottom so that viewers on the ground would see it correctly. If they could view it in scale, they would realize it was malformed. This example from the visual arts serves as a metaphor for the philosophical arts and the tendency of some philosophers to distort truth so that it appears accurate unless viewed from the proper angle

Wolfgang had entered the race quite unexpectedly, announcing his intention to run during a guest appearance on *Leonard Duke Live*, a popular ANN program watched by millions of devout news junkies. The three main candidates had held a pair of nationally-televised debates, with Wolf annihilating both Isenor and Simpson on each occasion. Leslie McKay's popularity in traditional political circles and Fuerst's own immense fame and corporate guise led to a rapid rise of legitimacy for the campaign, and now he stood on the cusp of greatness—ready to address his legion of fans and supporters as the most powerful man on the west coast.

"I love you, California!" Wolf shouted into the state-of-the-art microphone which sat atop a sturdy, oak podium—chosen by his publicist to project a definitive sense of strength. The fair-haired ex-jock then went into a hollow diatribe of grandiose promises to his constituents, poorly-written political-speak flowing from his lips effortlessly.

The election of Wolfgang Fuerst was the only significant global news story on this particular day, making the media coverage his victory speech received extensive beyond belief. An entire nation and millions of foreigners would witness his triumph, the bone-chillingly sinister consequences of his victory lost upon all but one man. And one man only.

«‹‹—››»

It's finally dark enough to make a move on the Solarite camp but Jenny's fallen asleep, so I open the driver's side door gently and skulk out of the car as quietly as possible. She really doesn't need to be here I guess and it's better if I do all the risky shit anyway. I look back to make sure she's still out cold as I start to make my way towards the compound.

They've only got one guard on duty, so I sneak up from behind the guy and put him in a sleeper hold until he's unconscious and then I steal his gun and say something totally badass under my breath[54]. There are about a dozen decent-sized tents on-site, so I go through them one-by-one looking for Iris and meet some pretty interesting characters in the process[55]. Eventually I get through them all and my stupid missing daughter is nowhere to be found so I go back to the guy I knocked out earlier, wake him up and ask him a few questions.

He doesn't have any answers. None that I like anyway. After I make sure he'll (probably) never be able to procreate he finally gives me the name of the guy that distributes the recruits to the Solarites' respective 'spiritual centers'. I ask for an address, but he doesn't know that, so I put him back in a sleeper hold again and knock him back out[56].

I make my way back to the car and Jenny's not there. I call out her name and nothing but silence greets me. There's some muffled shouting behind me so I guess that sleeper hold wore off already and that idiot guard is coming after me with some

---

[54] It wasn't badass at all, just a lame pun.

[55] False. None of them were even remotely interesting.

[56] From Wikipedia: Blood chokes, carotid restraint or sleeper holds, are a form of strangulation that compress one or both carotid arteries and/or the jugular veins without compressing the airway, hence causing cerebral ischemia and a temporary hypoxic condition in the brain. A well applied blood choke may lead to unconsciousness in a matter of seconds. Compared to strangulation with the hands, properly applied blood chokes require little physical strength.

backup. I fire the gun I stole from him into the air and shout out for Jenny one more time and then jump into the car and get the hell out of dodge.

《《——》》

I get back to the motel and order a bottle of vodka from room service. The bitch at the front desk tells me they don't have room service, so I walk to a gas station and buy a six pack of malt liquor. I get drunk in my room watching TV—premium cable baby.

A Wolfgang Fuerst movie called RACE RELATIONS is just ending; he loses the final stock car race to some black actor and they shake hands in the final shot all dramatic-like, so I guess they've become friends after some sort of tumultuousness in the preceding 89 minutes. Then a movie called CHILDREN OF BOKOR starts. It's set in the near future, I think, and takes place almost entirely in a depressing log cabin that's filled with brooding pre-teens dressed in rags. As far as I can tell there's some zombie-like virus that's fucked up the planet and kicks in when humans hit puberty so the villages or whatever send their kids to a remote destination—the depressing log cabin—to see which ones turn into zombies and which ones don't. The dialog is super weird and shit and one-by-one the kids start going through their metamorphosis and become monsters so dudes in orange nuclear suits that I guess have been watching them in the cabin have to come in and zap them with this ray gun that kills them instantly and the other kids all freak out at first but then it gets to be normal for them and they don't react at all which is probably supposed to be some kind of cultural commentary but maybe not. Eventually there's just two kids left—a boy and a girl—and they start to fall in love, and when the dude starts to turn into a zombie the orange crew comes in, but the chick gets in the way and they have to kill her first which makes the now-zombie dude sad and he cries zombie tears as he kneels by her corpse right before getting zapped with a ray gun too. Yup, that's how it ends—pretty lame.

After that they show some behind-the-scenes shit about that sexy-violent-weird medieval show I mentioned earlier. I'm not really a fan of that shit so I change the channel to the comedy station and there are three hipster guys sitting around laughing hysterically at something and then the one who must be the host gets them to calm down and lets us know that we're watching CINEMA JUNKYARD, which appears to be a show about these assholes making fun of bad movies. They just finished ridiculing SPACELAND CRUSADERS and up next is the film version of WAVEFRONT, a box office bomb of epic proportions deemed to be one of the worst motion pictures of all time. The host introduces a clip and it plays slightly out of focus for us which may or may not be intentional. I've never seen the thing obviously since it never existed in my dimension before the spacetime continuum got all messed up but I'm sure this piece of crap would've tanked in my universe as well. The scene they show is on a boat and it's all kinds of bad...

INT. SHIP'S LOWER DECK

Below deck, dozens of terrified soldiers sit in solemn silence as deafening thunder intermixes with the torrential downpour above. The camera slowly makes its way through the crowd, taking in a series of horrified expressions until finally settling on a stern-looking man exuding a supernatural sense of calm amidst the chaos. This is BADYN TAYLOR, professional streamball player and recent conscript of the Rodinian army. A hulking man with a shorn skull and several scars, he is dressed much like the other soldiers—light metallic armor covering his maroon wool trousers and an off-white tunic.

> SOLDIER #1
> Some baccha to calm your nerves, hoplite?

HE OFFERS BADYN A JUG OF ALCOHOL WITH SHAKING HANDS

> BADYN
> My nerves are just fine.

SOLDIER #1
Well to warm your innards
then? Mirovia appears to be
calling our souls to its
depths… I only pray the
cold takes mine before the
eocharchis find us… I've
heard they can eat upwards
of a dozen men before
getting full.

BADYN
Stories, amica, nothing
more.

SOLDIER #1
And what do you know of
Mirovia, hoplite?

BADYN
No more than you. I know
this ship is far too strong
and too powerful to be torn
apart by the likes of
Thoosa.

SOLDIER #1
That is blasphemy you speak,
hoplite! You dare mock a god
as we sit here in desperate
need of her mercy?!

BADYN
Mercy. If there's one thing
the gods are in short
supply of, it is most
certainly mercy.

SOLDIER #1
You speak as if you've been
in battle before and yet
your cuirass is blank.

HE TAPS BADYN'S CHEST PLATE
WITH HIS INDEX FINGER.
BADYN GRABS HIS HAND AND
GIVES THE DRUNKARD A
MENACING GLARE.

BADYN
My cuirass may be barren.

> HE TURNS TO LOOK OUT OF A
> WINDOW, SEEING A SERIES OF
> LIGHTNING STRIKES.

> But I have been in many a
> battle, stulte.

EXT. TANIT COLISEUM (FLASHBACK)—LIGHTNING
STREAKS ACROSS THE SKY AS AN AERIAL SHOT
ABSORBS A LARGE STREAMBALL STADIUM FILLED
WITH RAUCOUS FANS… PAN DOWN TO THE ON-
FIELD ACTION.

Donning a mud-covered uniform (centu-
rion-style helmet with football-style
facemask, black robe with the numeral
XI on it, gold chest plate, brown
leather boots), Badyn Taylor receives a
pass from a teammate (a discus-shaped
object) and begins to run down the
field, knocking over several opposing
players. Several fans cheer loudly as
the skies begin to open up and rain
descends from the heavens.

Badyn crosses a thick white line on the
turf and waits for two of his teammates
brandishing large metallic shields to
catch up to him and join together to
form a protective safeguard for him

prior to entering the offensive zone. The two clipeis move forward as three opposing cataphs advance upon them with clubs as soon as they cross the white line, battering them viciously.

Badyn yells "Pugna!" and the clipeis thrust their shields upward as he runs between them, past the cataphs. He then jukes a masked cliban, who slips in a puddle as the rain begins to fall heavier, and drops his whip-like weapon—allowing Badyn to heave the streamball through a ring-shaped goal, producing a bright green light as it breaches the target. Several horns go off and the crowd cheers as Badyn celebrates with his teammates.

INT. TOREMS LOCKER ROOM—SEVERAL PLAYERS ARE SHOWERING IN THE TEAM TEPIDARIUM WHILE OTHERS ARE CHANGING BACK INTO THEIR STREET CLOTHES, INCLUDING BADYN TAYLOR

                    TOREMS PLAYER
            That was one hell of a play
            you made on that last
            caedo, Taylor.

BADYN
Thank you. I got lucky
their cliban slipped.

TOREMS PLAYER
Yes, Thoosa was looking out
for you on that one,
drowning the field in rain
just before you entered
their zone…

BADYN
Luck and hocus pocus are
two very different things,
socius. HE PATS HIS TEAM-
MATE ON THE BACK AND WALKS
OUT OF THE LOCKER ROOM. You
played well today. Enjoy
your evening.

TOREMS PLAYER
You as well, ducer. You as
well.

Badyn makes his way into the hallway,
stopping to sign an autograph for a
young fan. He is approached by two men

dressed in black tunics, dark cappello
romanos and translucent eyebands. They
are ZOTICUS and AESOP, agents in the
Rodinian secret police.

          AESOP
   Mr. Taylor?

          BADYN
   Yes?

          AESOP
   (PRESENTING HIS IDENTIFICATION)
   My name is Aesop Jennings,
   this is my colleague
   Zoticus Bartlett. We were
   wondering if we might have
   a word with you. In
   private.

          BADYN
   Anything for the
   Frumentarii.

INT. MAIN CABIN OF THE NEPTUNE (BACK TO
PRESENT). BADYN AWAKENS FROM A LIGHT SLEEP.
IT IS NOW DAYTIME AND HE LOOKS OUT THE
WINDOW TO SEE A CALM SEA STRETCHING OUT FOR
AN ETERNITY BEFORE HIM. THE SOLDIER STANDS
AND SHAKES THE DRUNKARD WHO'D MOCKED HIM
THE PREVIOUS NIGHT, WAKING HIM UP.

> BADYN
> Good morning, amica. It
> appears we've survived the
> storm.

> SOLDIER #1
> (GROGGILY)
> Praise to Thoosa!

> BADYN
> Your superstitions won't do
> you any good where we're
> headed, ecc.

> SOLDIER #1
> On the contrary, hoplite—
> that is *exactly* what
> we'll need.

Taylor walks away, towards the staircase leading towards the main deck.

          SOLDIER #2
Don't you know who that
is, Miles?

          SOLDIER #1
No. Should I?

          SOLDIER #2
You've never heard of
Badyn Taylor? Led the
RSL in caedos last
season?

          SOLDIER #1
I'm more of a halteredon
fan myself actually.

          SOLDIER #2
Of course, you are.

SOLDIER #1
What's this superstar doing
here with us on this fool's
errand then if he's such a
big deal?

SOLDIER #2
No one knows… It's a mystery.

After the clip those three idiots make fun of WAVEFRONT and Solarism for a while but none of their jokes are any good, so I switch the channel over to the news and pass out during a story about President Thompson's impending trip to California and how Governor Fuerst is providing his private security team to assist in the visit[57]. This seems pretty important to the plot but I'm too drunk to take in many details. Sorry about that.

《《——》》

While I'm asleep I have a super-vivid dream about a random guy who decides to start killing off homeless people by making poisoned sandwiches and passing them out in a city that's either Seattle or Vancouver and he ends up getting away with it for like a year but then he gets bored and starts trying to poison drug dealers and criminals and such like he's a vigilante or whatever and eventually he poisons a mafia boss' little daughter and a bunch of goons take him to a warehouse and skin him alive with a potato peeler. Ouch.

---

[57] From AllTheTropes.Wikia.com: 'Coincidental Broadcast/Laconic' - A helpful hint is dispensed by the TV.

I wake up in the late morning and the TV is still tuned into the news channel and it's another story about Thompson visiting L.A. so I try and pay attention this time but then the phone rings and when I pick it up it's Jenny on the other end of the line. Interesting.

"Where are you?" I ask her.

"At the office," she says, matter-of-factly.

"What the hell happened to you last night?"

"You were gone when I woke up, so I just took off. Figured you bailed or got killed or something."

"How did you get back to L.A. without a car though?"

"Hitchhiker's Leg Trope. I'm a chick in her twenties with nice legs so it was pretty easy to execute. You're not the only one negotiating this fifth wall dynamic now, big guy."

"Nicely done."

"So, did you find your daughter there or what?"

"No, she wasn't there."

"So, what now?"

"I got the name of the guy who coordinates the dissemination of new recruits to their spiritual... whatever centers. I'll be heading out to find him shortly."

"What's his name?"

My mind goes blank for a few seconds and Jenny gives me an annoying Valley Girl remark but then it pops back into my head, so I tell her, "Scott Nelson."

"Scott Nelson?"

"Yeah."

"As in Blake Wilson's manager?"

"Huh?"

"That's the name of Blake Wilson's manager."

"The actor?"

"Yeah, he's big into Solarism—how do you not know that?"

"Dramatic Ignorance."

"That's too easy."

"Dramatic Irony?"

"Sure. So, when are we going to meet with Scott Nelson?"

"It's 'we' again, is it?"

"Well you're alive, aren't you?"

"More or less."

"So, our deal is still intact then—we find your daughter and get my story, cool?"

"Cool. You have any idea where we can find this guy?"

"You watching TV?"

"Yeah, the news."

"Well turn it to channel nine. Blake Wilson's on *The Patty Winters Show* right now and I'm guessing Nelson is there with him."

I find the remote in my bed and switch it over to the program in question as I give Jenny directions to my motel. "When can you pick me up?"

"On my way. Be there in ten."

Just as I hang up the phone my tablet springs to life like something out of a cartoon movie about enchanted brooms. The LiveStory app loads itself and starts to project its text up against the wall in a hazy blue beam in a font that I think is from the sans-serif family, hammering out its narrative in a machine gun-like typewriter manner that I quickly realize is totally in sync with what I'm watching on TV, like a close caption teleprompter or whatever. So, I guess now all the timelines and dimensions and shit we've been juggling are all starting to match up, which is of course terribly exciting, isn't it?[58]

---

[58] Meh.

CHAPTER XVIII

An electronic APPLAUSE sign flickered on and off. Nearly two hundred studio audience members obliged the mechanical command and erupted into a bland, obligatory chorus of hands gently striking hands.

"Welcome back!" Patty Winters enthusiastically proclaimed. She stared directly into Camera 3 with her trademark gaze–intense yet alluring–just as she had done for longer than she'd care to admit. A recent Botox injection meant that her sleek, angular face could barely move, seemingly frozen completely still as she spoke through a pair of incredibly thin lips–mere slivers of peach-colored flesh.

Once a well-respected, world-renowned journalist, Patty Winters was now just another vapid talking head treading water in a cluttered pool of mediocrity. Celebrities would sit next to her and plug their latest projects while she nodded her head vacantly and read questions from index cards provided by Armani-clad publicists. She was a mere shadow of her former self, yet her popularity was now greater than ever–housewives and soccer moms adoring her harmlessly banal, righteously pleasant daytime talk show.

Occasionally, Patty Winters would feel the kind of fruit-less longing that effete philosophy majors grieve over on grotesquely verbose online blogs. A steady stream of antidepressants provided to her by a manager—or maybe an assistant or lawyer or even a fan, it was impossible to know for sure—always kept her within striking distance of the mind frame she needed to be in to effectively perform the mundane tasks associated with her obscenely-well-paying job, however.

Now though, as she sat staring at another incredibly handsome actor with bright white teeth and cheekbones so high that they nearly touched his scalp, a rare sense of purpose coursed through Patty Winters' weak, weathered body. A sense of *life* seemed to be awakening from a deep slumber as she began the second segment of her exclusive interview with one of Hollywood's most successful actors.

She heard her own raspy-yet-soothing voice begin to speak as words were uttered that had not even entered her brain, an autopilot having long ago taken command of the controls inside Patty Winters' once-sharp mind.

"We're here with Hollywood superstar Blake Wilson, who just finished telling us about his latest project, the soon-to-be-hit film *Deadly Games*. Really sounds like a great movie."

Almost interrupting—he was notorious for stepping on his costars' lines—Wilson responded with the zeal of a rookie quarterback running onto the field to lead his team on their first drive in a championship game.

"Thanks, Patty, *Deadly Games* was a lot of fun to make as I said earlier. Really a great cast, a great script, and a fantastic director. Malcolm Gilmour is very talented, and it was a thrill to work with him."

Blake Wilson had been one of Hollywood's most bankable leading men for nearly fifteen years, ever since the release of his first blockbuster, a fighter pilot movie entitled *Air Commandos*. In the stylish, oft-parodied action movie that seemed dated within months of its release, Wilson had played a talented, yet troubled naval aviator forced to single-handedly rescue an entire battalion of POWs in war-torn Bosnia after a freak lightning storm rendered his fleet-mates' planes completely useless[59].

After *Air Commandos*, Wilson had played the lead in several romantic comedies, straight-forward action films, and anything else that didn't require his mediocre acting skills to seem too out-of-place. Wilson's most famous role was that of renegade police lieutenant Jake Reign in the highly-profitable *Reign Dance* series, a film franchise that was currently undergoing casting for what would be a fifth installment. All four previous movies had combined to earn nearly two billion dollars at the box office, with Wilson's salary for Part V reportedly in the $30-35 million range.

Constantly pursued by the paparazzi, the dashing playboy had recently settled down and, even more shockingly, begun taking on more serious roles as his good looks began to fade and his supernatural charm

---

59 From Wikipedia: Astraphobia, also known as astrapophobia, brontophobia, keraunophobia, or tonitrophobia is an abnormal fear of thunder and lightning, a type of specific phobia. It is a treatable phobia that both humans and animals can develop. The term astraphobia is composed of the words ἀστραπή (astrape; lightning) and φόβος (phobos; fear).

began to wear thin. *Deadly Games* was his most ambitious project to date, and he, or at least his handlers, desperately needed the film to succeed, already looking ahead to the days when Blake Wilson would no longer be able to play Jake Reign-type roles.

"Great, so everyone watching be sure to go out and see *Deadly Games* this coming weekend at your local theater," Patty Winters proclaimed, overselling the line badly. Unexpectedly realizing this, she continued, self-hatred now gnawing away at her innards like a rabid chipmunk.

A consummate professional, the syndicated television star continued her interview.

"Now, your professional life is clearly going amazingly well. We all know that you and your wife, actress Mallory Dundas, are incredibly happy together and you'll be celebrating your one-year anniversary next month."

"Really? Yikes, thanks for the reminder!"

The contrived one-liner resulted in a monotonous cackle raining down from the studio audience. A frumpy homemaker in the second row loudly professed her love for Wilson, a giddy elderly woman echoing the same sentiment immediately thereafter.

"Haha. Seriously though, tell us what else you have going on in your amazing life." Patty Winters now found herself choking back a volatile self-loathing which churned densely within the depths of a waking subconscious.

"Well I've been really busy with my volunteer work lately. I'm an active member of C.U.R.E.D. N.O.W. as you know."

"Right, Celebrities United for Reading and Education in Developing Nations all Over the World."

"Exactly."

The sheer absurdity of Wilson's synthetic pride nearly caused Patty Winters to vomit.

"I was recently in Zambia to oversee the construction of the latest learning center we've set up for young Africans to... um... be taught how to break out of the cycle of poverty that has engulfed the whole continent. While there, I befriended a young peasant named Kupela, which means 'Last Child' in the Tumbuka dialect, and I couldn't help but thinking that we can *all* be doing more to help others in this harsh, unfair world."

Wilson paused, as if he expected his interviewer to chime in with a comment canonizing his noble endeavors. He was instead met with a cold, determined glare from a woman suddenly experiencing a dramatic crisis of conscience.

In an illogical instant, Patty Winters was decades younger and bursting with journalistic integrity. Her head now spinning, the star of *The Patty Winters Show* stared down at one of the pale blue index cards she had been given earlier in the day. On this particular card was written a series of topics that were deemed strictly off-limits for this particular interview by the omnipotent powers that be.

At the top of this list was the name of the controversial new age religion Blake Wilson had been a member of for several years now: The Church of Solarism.

Channeling her former self, Patty Winters cleared her throat and abruptly ended the previous topic of discussion. "That's really great, Blake, good luck with all of that."

The diminutive heartthrob appeared to be wholly taken aback by the sternness of the famous talk show host's tone.

"You're also heavily involved with the... Church of Solarism. Why don't you tell us about that? America is dying to know about your spiritual side, right ladies?"

More raucous cackling and high-pitched squealing from suspended adolescents erupted as Patty turned to the crowd invitingly, raising her sickeningly-thin arms in mock triumph.

Wilson looked helplessly towards his bewildered manager at the side of the stage. Scott Nelson was able to return only an anxious glance and a nervous shrug.

A mischievousness look suddenly overtook Wilson's flawless face, his deep brown eyes filled with devilish glee.

Out of nowhere, an incredibly-excited Blake Wilson leapt up on the plush sofa on which he had been sitting and started playing air guitar as he proclaimed: "Solarism rocks!" He did a theatrical dismount from the studio couch and added: "I just love it! I love The Church of Solarism!" as he landed.

An astonished studio audience struggled to laugh at Wilson's insane antics. At the side of the stage, a man in an expensive navy-blue suit held his hands over his head, his mouth wide open, awash in disbelief.

Patty Winters, too, was aghast at the response she had received from such an innocent-sounding question. She had merely hoped to be able to cause even a little bit of discomfort in one of her guests for once, but the situation had turned on her like a dynamite-laden boomerang. In her still-lucid state, she quickly realized that this appearance would soon be talked about at water coolers and in coffee shops nationwide. The clip of Wilson dancing crazily upon her set would live for an eternity on the Internet. It would be referenced by late night comedians for weeks to come. *This is ratings gold!*[60]

After a carefully-paced, uncomfortable moment, Patty looked back into Camera 3 and forced herself to speak, her intrepid, weathered face radiating a strange kind of fractured regality that was at once endearing and bothersome.

"Alright, um... well there you have it America—Blake Wilson is in love with The Church of Solarism. And he plays a mean air guitar. We'll be right back."

The lights atop all four in-studio cameras dimmed as a commercial promoting a new miracle fabric softener went to air.

Wilson stood perfectly still, like a statuesque... statue. He stared blankly out at his silent audience prior to slowly making his way off of the set, grinning sheepishly at no one in particular.

《《《———》》》

Jenny pulls up in one of those tiny rent-by-the-hour smart car things I can barely fit into and she's got some god-awful techno music blaring that gives me an instant headache. I yell at her to turn it the fuck down, but she speeds away before I can even shut

---

[60] From Wikipedia: In the arts, maximalism, a reaction against minimalism, is an esthetic of excess and redundancy.

the door behind me and all-of-a-sudden we're on the highway racing towards the studio where *The Patty Winters Show* is shot every afternoon, airing live from coast-to-coast[61].

I try and make small talk with Jenny but she's pretty into this techno song that's playing and I'm not even sure she hears me ask about the weather forecast and such. We pass a horse & buggy, a miniature Sherman tank with a giant cork jammed in the barrel of its main gun and a futuristic-looking sports car being driven by some asshole in a top hat on our way to the studio.

«‹‹——››»

When we get to the studio Jenny flashes her press credential at the parking attendant and he makes a bad pass at her that all three of us cringe at right before he waves us into the visitor lot. She does a shitty job of pulling into an open spot and then we're speed-walking towards the main entrance.

A half-awake security guard asks to see Jenny's press credential and he hits on her too after noticing how hot she is, but this guy's game is even worse than the dude in the parking lot so it's a pretty short conversation and then we're strolling down a bright hallway littered with photos of Patty Winters sitting with famous people in her studio, smiling brightly[62].

Jenny asks a network page where Blake Wilson is and he points at something behind us so we turn to see a massive horde of people moving in our direction. A couple of hulking security guards are shielding this porcelain-skinned caricature of an elfish

---

[61] From Wikipedia: Retroactive continuity, or retcon for short] is a literary device in which new information is added to already established facts in the continuity of a fictional work.

[62] From Wikipedia: Stream-of-consciousness writing is usually regarded as a special form of interior monologue and is characterized by associative leaps in thought and lack of some or all punctuation.

beauty king from a bunch of screaming girls and autograph hounds. I try and ask Jenny what the plan is exactly but before I can get the words out of my mouth she's loudly asking Wilson's handlers, including Scott Nelson, about the Church and how they kidnap and brainwash wannabe actors and shit and they obviously don't like that very much so the bodyguard dudes focus their attention on us as some broad who I guess is a publicist or something barks out a couple of sentences that pretty much amount to 'no comment' and then there's a flash of orange light and we're back out in the parking lot. Everything that just happened seems like a dream or some kind of clinically-induced hallucination. This whole thing could be come to think of it. Or maybe I'm a brain in a vat. Maybe you are too. Are you reading this right now? How can you be sure? Maybe you're reading something else or maybe you're reading nothing at all? It's possible, isn't it? Maybe *this* is the book within the book and not that other one we've been reading... Speaking of which...

CHAPTER XIX

Heinrich Fuerst tipped his taxi driver well, wishing the talkative grad student luck on his upcoming exam as he flung a duffle bag over his shoulder and gazed up at the most magnificent dwelling he had ever seen.

The Governor's Mansion did not seem to be as well-guarded as Heinrich had expected. A lifetime of inspecting buildings for potential threats and weaknesses had given the aspiring tyrant a sixth sense for effective security apparatus, and he could tell just by looking at the exterior of his brother's new home that a new system would soon have to be installed in the very near future.

The lone sentinel on duty on this particular morning was quickly subdued with a highly-effective knockout potion Heinrich had recently developed in his private laboratory. Fuerst had grown accustomed to the habit of carrying with him at all times a water pistol which contained the non-fatal elixir. This marked the first time that he'd been able to use it outside of his makeshift testing facilities, and he beamed with pride at the remarkable effectiveness his latest creation had enjoyed during its first field test.

Although he was now well into his 50s, Fuerst still possessed cat-like reflexes and dynamic agility. After rendering the guard unconscious, Fuerst proceeded to negotiate his way through the mansion with the ability of a gymnast-turned-spy, skillfully avoiding the security cameras which were stationed in fairly obvious locations throughout the vast abode.

As he finally reached the governor's home office, he found his fraternal twin exercising with a massive dumbbell before a gargantuan portrait of the California coastline.

"Guten Morgen, Bruder," Heinrich proclaimed upon entering the room.

Good Morning, Brother.

As a ninety-pound free-weight fell to the ground, the hulking, gallant figure that had recently conquered the political world was taken aback, violently—a feeling he was definitely not accustomed to.

"Heinrich..." Wolfgang muttered with a small hint of disbelief buried beneath an avalanche of terror.

"We have much to discuss... Your Excellency."

Wolfgang walked towards Heinrich cautiously, his gaze never relenting from an intense transfixion upon his long-lost brother.

"Yes, I suppose we do, don't we..." he eventually replied, almost reluctantly. They shook hands, Wolf refraining from administering his normal vicelike grip as he felt suddenly weak for the first time in his adult life.

The two men spoke for several hours, Heinrich putting forth the plan he had concocted which would amalgamate his own resources—a vast network of underground fascists and white supremacists fronted by the increasingly-popular new age religion that their father had founded—with the mainstream political power now possessed by

165

Wolfgang. The joint effort would undoubtedly lead to their fulfillment of their familial destiny, and Heinrich brimmed with excitement as he recounted the multi-year plan.

Wolfgang's worst fears had at long last come to fruition. His domineering, malevolent brother had re-entered his life, immediately seizing control of it and imposing his ironclad will upon his intellectual subordinate. *The dream is over… The nightmare has now begun.*

The prestigious office Wolf had held oh-so-briefly was now controlled by the most efficacious neo-Nazi the world had ever known.

《《——》》

Jenny is quiet again as we drive away from the TV studio and I'm honestly not sure where the hell we're going but I guess it doesn't really matter since we don't have a plan as far as I can tell and the Scott Nelson lead obviously didn't amount to much. The cars and buildings we passed all take on a smeared, neon-pastel-like appearance which adds credence to my aforementioned hallucination theory.

I'm about to say something super important to the story when that stupid magic tablet springs to life and shoots the car stereo with a ray of lighting or something and Jenny starts screaming at the top of her lungs, swerving in and out of traffic and prompting several cars to honk violently as they narrowly avoid hitting us. Eventually she stops screaming and we're driving straight. That's when some British guy starts talking at us from out of the car speakers and after about a tenth of a second, I realize he's reading the LiveStory novel I lost control of several thousand words ago.

CHAPTER XX

Sitting in a dark, shadow-riddled basement, Heinrich Fuerst patiently awaited the arrival of his famous brother. Declan Farrelly sat with him, polishing his antique Mauser P27 pistol with a rag he had brought with him in case such a delay in their scheduled meeting might occur.

A headline reading '28th AMENDMENT RATIFIED– FOREIGNERS NOW ALLOWED TO SERVE AS PREZ' stared up at them, inscribed across the top of a page in a popular national newspaper which was folded neatly atop the cheap, plastic table at which they sat.

While it should've been on the cover of the tabloid-style publication, the article in fact appeared on page four of *American Newsday*.

For several days every conceivable media outlet in the United States had been focused entirely on a story involving a controversial half-time performance at pro football's championship game. An aging pop star had exposed his penis during a dance routine, prompting American Broadcast Network executives to cut to dead air while nearly a billion people watched, horrified[63].

---

[63] From Wikipedia: Wikipedia is a free online encyclopedia that allows its users to edit almost any article. Wikipedia is the largest and most popular general

The next day the talentless singer, who had recently joined a mysterious new age religion that was beginning to gain notoriety through a series of well-placed testimonials, was found dead of a gunshot wound to the head and the murder weapon was soon found in the trunk of a European-made car belonging to ABN president Hershel Weinberg. The media had gone into absolute frenzy following the massive scandal, making the impending constitutional alteration a mere side note in the annals of American news coverage[64].

Heinrich beamed with self-satisfaction at having orchestrated the elaborate distraction which had made a vital component of his plan to erect his Pan-Aryan Reich so easy to accomplish. The millions of dollars his brother had covertly spent in bribing politicians from all walks of life would easily be recouped by the advance Stonefish Publishing was providing for the rights to Wolfgang's upcoming autobiography[65].

"Where can he be?" Declan asked, his uncle's firearm now spectacularly pristine.

"He will be here, don't worry."

Since reentering his brother's life, Heinrich had moved

---

reference work on the Internet and is ranked among the ten most popular websites. Wikipedia is owned by the nonprofit Wikimedia Foundation.

[64] Wikipedia was launched on January 15, 2001, by Jimmy Wales and Larry Sanger. Sanger coined its name, a portmanteau of wiki and encyclopedia. It was only in the English language initially, but it quickly developed similar versions in other languages which differ in content and in editing practices.

[65] Wikipedia is not considered a credible source. Wikipedia is increasingly used by people in the academic community, from freshman students to professors, as an easily accessible tertiary source for information about anything and everything. However, citation of Wikipedia in research papers may be considered unacceptable, because Wikipedia is not considered a credible or authoritative source.

quickly to configure the ingenious plan which would fulfill their family's blood oath. Upon gaining access to Wolfgang's extensive financial resources he had been able to stabilize and then expand the United Aryan Front's operational scope, injecting substantial, legitimate cash flow into the underground organization.

The multiple front companies Heinrich had set up around the country through Wolf's extensive real estate holdings now owned several large plots of land which were now serving as training centers for the growing legions of UAF soldiers. A bankrupt bottling factory in Delaware had also recently been purchased and would soon begin brewing the Wolff-Glahn Concoction in mass quantities.

The crown jewel in Heinrich's conglomerate was undoubtedly the Church of Solarism however. It had been in the wake of the now-infamous Day of Reckoning that Fuerst had realized that Robert Alexander Stephens had been apt in his appropriation of religion in his quest for procurement of an Aryan Utopia. By reintegrating the dogmatic principles his father had taught him into a well-designed, theatrical religion, his impending empire would be able to distribute a spiritual opiate to the masses, using its principles as a means of advancing his political agenda to its utmost.

Heinrich had originally thought that his father's tinkering with Sun Worshiping dogma had been the result of some kind of mental illness that had precipitated his untimely demise. Now, decades later, he felt he fully understood what Reinhard had been up to in his final years.

Faith was of grand importance to any society. Its absence had been why the Soviet Union had collapsed, why the Third Reich had lasted merely a dozen years. Exploiting humanity's need for belief in a greater power would ensure that Reich No. 4 would indeed last a millennia, if not longer.

In addition to replacing Christianity as the official faith of the western hemisphere in the coming years, Solarism would also be used to recruit new members to the UAF. Aspiring actors were prime targets due to their extreme prevalence and the ease with which their delusional aspirations could be manipulated.

With a vague dogma which incorporated a ludicrous assortment of solar deities from throughout history, just as the Order of the Black Sun had done, Solarism was compelling only thanks to the increasing prevalence of Wolf's film industry acquaintances joining the religion, thus making the church attractive to aspiring stars and starlets, of which there were thousands upon thousands in Los Angeles County alone.

Highly-susceptible to the brain washing technique Reinhard had passed on to Heinrich on his deathbed, known simply as 'The Treatment' within the upper echelon of the UAF, the young men and women who flocked to the church were at once invaluable and expendable—perfect foot soldiers in a growing army of white supremacists who would soon carry out the most horrific act of domestic terrorism in American history[66].

---

[66] From TVTropes.org: A portmanteau of anvil and delicious, anvilicious describes a writer's and/or director's use of an artistic element, be it line of dialogue, visual motif, or plot point, to so unsubtly convey a particular message that they may as well etch it onto an anvil and drop it on your head.

Now, as he sat waiting for Wolfgang to arrive at the Church of Solarism's headquarters, Heinrich went over his elaborate plot again in his mind, calculating for any and all possible scenarios that might disrupt the Fuerst Brothers' ascension to supreme power.

The State of California had indeed prospered under Wolfgang's leadership, and, as a result, he now was a major national political figure. Beloved by both conservatives and liberals alike, the charismatic movie star had made rumblings about running for president in the next election, but the constitution had forbidden the foreign-born Adonis from doing so. Now, with the latest amendment being passed, a non-traditional path to the White House was already being cleared, with Heinrich's diabolical genius being utilized to full effect.

"Perhaps he is lost. Has he even seen this building yet, Heinrich?" Declan asked, candidly.

"Yes, of course he has seen it," Heinrich snapped at his longtime companion, anxiously looking at his wristwatch again prior to trying to reach Wolf on his cell phone.

"Blast, I can't get a signal down here..." Fuerst lamented.

At long last Wolfgang's heavy steps could be heard descending the staircase leading to the hidden basement chamber where Heinrich and Declan had been waiting.

"Sorry," Wolfgang stated, unapologetically. "Traffic."

California's governor sat at the small, spherical table, directly facing the two men with whom his destiny was now intertwined. He sipped gently on an extra-large, designer-brand coffee, his dark blue, nylon tracksuit suggesting he was either on his way from or to the stately Furious Fitness workout complex he had opened at the height of his box office glory in the '80s. Shortly after winning his second election by a historic margin, a national referendum had passed which revoked the two-term limit imposed on state governors. It was a perfect test-run for their 28th Amendment scheme.

Wolf's second term had in fact been an unmitigated success as unemployment rates reached a record low in California while crime had fallen dramatically and taxes had somehow been lowered. With the top political advisors in the world on his payroll, Wolf had been nearly deified in California, at least in the eyes of mainstream media members, many of whom were also secretly in Governor Fuerst's employ.

A small group of highly-vocal naysayers loudly continued to accuse the former boxer of corrupt dealings however. They believed him to be linked with several organized crime syndicates who had been able to break up key unions in the Golden State and thus allow for Fuerst's historic Employment Reform Act to pass without impediment.

The protestors who believed him to have struck a one-time deal with the mafia could not possibly imagine the full scope of Fuerst's malevolence however.

"It is done brother—the amendment was ratified. We are now one step closer to realizing our goals," Heinrich said, sliding the newspaper across a glossy plastic tabletop.

Wolf picked it up, nodding approvingly. "Good, good… This business with the executive at ABN and the black singer though," Wolfgang added, sheepishly.

"What of it?" Declan chimed in.

"I'm just not… certain that such an act was needed. It had no real bearing on any of our plans or activities. Many lives were ruined unnecessarily."

Heinrich tilted his neck, a loud *crack* ringing out as boiling adrenaline suddenly surged through him. His brother had been questioning his actions with greater frequency as of late, and the megalomaniacal master-mind did not view dissent auspiciously. The United Aryan Front's tyrannical leader stared angrily at his mighty twin, almost through him–as if he were an uncooperative magic eye 3-D puzzle.

"Wolfgang… the more the press is distracted by fool-ishness such as this television executive scandal, the less likely they are to vigorously investigate the… less-than-reputable means by which our friends in Washington were able to push this motion through. You must under-stand this." Heinrich's tone was condescending, as if he were addressing a petulant child.

"Yes, of course," Wolf muttered, embarrassed.

"Plus, it was only a Jew and some Jigaboo that really suffered," Declan chimed in.

"Exactly–two less we'll have to worry about in the coming years," Heinrich added. "Now, onto more pressing matters–the Australian actor you brought to us–Gilmour. We will need him to carry out a very integral part of our plan in the coming months. He still has strong ties at the Vatican, does he not?"

Wolf nodded, meekly.

"Good. We will need him to make a film version of the Passion Play that vilifies Hebrews and then himself make public claims regarding the validity of the Elders of Zion's world domination conspiracy... This will ultimately serve to both discredit Christianity and incense the Israelites to just the right degree, allowing *our* new religion to begin to permeate the mass consciousness as it will not have the baggage of the Old-World faiths. The Muslims are obviously capable of making their religion look foolish all on their own."

The three men discussed Heinrich's extensive, diabolical plot for the next two hours, the blood flowing through Wolf's veins growing ever cooler. He eventually began to tremble violently as a profound chill overtook him.

‹‹‹——›››

We pull off the highway and then suddenly we're in a giant parking garage. Jenny pulls into a spot between two massive SUVs and tries to turn the stereo off. The British guy reading the story to us gets pissed off and tells her to knock it off. "Fuck you!" Jenny screams at the stereo and then she starts punching the dashboard for a while until her fists are bleeding. Then she stops, and a tsunami of silence deluges the car as we just sit there for what feels like forever, staring down at the stereo control panel. The British guy laughs for a few seconds, like a cartoon supervillain, and then he asks us if he can get back to the story. We nod at the console. He clears his throat and continues...

CHAPTER XXI

Heinrich Fuerst strolled confidently down a nondescript corridor located on the top floor of the Governor's Mansion, effortlessly whistling a nineteenth century folk song the name of which he did not know nor, truth be told, care to know.

The aging Vietnam veteran casually entered his brother's office, forgoing the generic pleasantries usually associated with one's entrance into a given room in favor of issuing a profoundly terse statement which caused Wolfgang to look up from the governmental ordinances he'd been fruitlessly staring at for the better part of an hour.

"You are to be named Vice President Mason's successor on the morrow," Heinrich stated, unabashed satisfaction permeating each and every syllable. A series of sexual misconduct allegations levied against the V.P. by women and young boys on the Fuerst payroll had indeed proven to be a high-yield investment for Heinrich and his long-term plans. "A private jet is now waiting to take you to Washington, the ceremony set to take place first thing in the morning so as to not interrupt President Thompson's speaking tour... It has worked out perfectly, simply perfectly–the venue he is scheduled to speak at tomorrow afternoon is one of the three we targeted for Phase One of the operation, our own people heavily involved with security protocols... Fate is truly on our side, lieber Bruder!"

After a long, silent moment, Heinrich produced a pair of expensive cigars from his lapel pocket, lit them both, and gradually made his way to Wolfgang's desk. He deliberately forced his colossal sibling to wait for the communist-made nicotine vessel to be placed in his enormous, Cro-Magnon-esque hand.

"It's unfolding just as we planned," Heinrich said after taking a deep, pleasurable puff. "Soon you will be called upon to the most powerful office in the world and from there the plan I have devised to launch the Pan-Aryan Reich that our father dreamed of will be carried out.[67]"

Wolfgang looked down upon the silver-plated pistol which sat upon the top of his desk at all times. He wondered if he were to kill his brother, right then and there, if it would be enough to stop the humming motor of evil which had just switched into a higher gear. This was an act that was well beyond his means however, as the psychological training he'd undergone as a child strictly forbade him from causing harm to the smaller, weaker blood relative to whom he was now functionally enslaved.

"Yes, I believe Father would be pleased," Wolf replied at long last, reluctantly sucking upon his cigar.

Governor Fuerst cleared his throat, unnecessarily, and continued: "Are you quite sure it would not be prudent though... to wait for the ink to dry on my new business

---

[67] From Wikipedia: Exposition is one of four rhetorical modes (also known as modes of discourse), along with description, argumentation, and narration.

cards before we proceed with the next phase?" he asked, in a childlike manner. "This is all happening rather fast."

Insulted, Heinrich extinguished his cigar upon Wolf's vintage Brazilian rosewood desk, glaring tellingly into his famous sibling's eyes.

"Do you not understand the need for expedience in this issue? The political blitzkrieg we have worked so tirelessly to set up is of paramount importance to the eventual conquest of this continent and the subjection of all those who stand in our way... It is only through a precise, expertly-timed execution of the operation that we will be successful. If there is time for resistance to grow regarding your appointment by President Thompson, then his decision might be overruled by the Senate...[68] If this happens, then the assassination itself is of no use to us, and the hundreds of UAF soldiers who have been training all these years to carry out Operation Tacitus will have no purpose for living. Is this what you want brother?? An army of noble Aryans reduced to the level of mere custodians? Men that would *die* for either of us at a moment's notice, men who have devoted their minds and souls to our cause betrayed, abandoned by the great Wolfgang Fuerst as a means of... contrived cowardice??"

The inherently rhetorical content of Heinrich's bombastic tirade left Wolf speechless.

Now unable to look his brother in the eye, 'Furious' Fuerst looked at the silver gun on his desk once again, wondering if turning it on himself might accomplish anything.

---

[68] From Wikipedia: An ellipsis (plural ellipses; from the Ancient Greek: ἔλλειψις, élleipsis, "omission" or "falling short") is a series of dots (typically three, such as "...") that usually indicates an intentional omission of a word, sentence, or whole section from a text without altering its original meaning.

‹‹‹‹——››››

"What now then?" Jenny asks me, her tone that of utter defeat.

"Well, I guess we try and stop the Fuerst Brothers from assassinating President Thompson," I sigh, realizing that we're already well into the third act of the story somehow.

"And how do we do that exactly?"

"Well, given the First Law of Metafictional Thermodynamics[69], we can assume that they'll try and pull off the assassination at that same appearance we've been hearing about on the radio and on TV the last few chapters. So, let's head to that convention center where Thompson is giving his speech and find the assholes they sent to whack him. I'm jonesing for a hot dog too—do you know if they sell those there?"

Jenny starts to sob so I guess she's thinking about the Big Picture shit that bummed her out before. "So, there are laws you need to follow in this bullshit meta-world you say we live in?" she asks me.

"Of course—it's just like anything else. Relativity, Gravity, Thou Shall Not Covet Thy Neighbor's Shit, Occam's Razor, Mass-Energy Equivalence, the Sliding Scale of Fourth Wall Hardness, Bellisario's Maxim—it's all the same nonsense."

Jenny shakes her head and mutters something about love and compassion and every feeling she's ever felt being bogus but then she undergoes some timely Character Derailment and accepts everything I've told her complicity. She grabs the enchanted computer tablet and asks me if it's our MacGuffin.

"That would explain why we can't get rid of it," I say. "It's also in keeping with Clarke's Third Law—Any sufficiently advanced technology… is indistinguishable from magic."

---

[69] For any fictional system, the sum of the mass in the system and the energy in the system is a constant.

"What about your daughter? Could she be considered a MacGuffin as well?"

"Huh?"

"Your *motivation*, Shane, ostensibly the whole reason for everything that's happening here. You're trying to find her, right? And I'm probably just here for eye candy in case some idiot producer in this town options the film rights?"

"Yeah, that and I guess it's a sequel, so I need a partner now or something. Either way it's been cool having you around. Full disclosure, I've thought about you whilst jerking off a couple of times already."

"Sweet. Thanks."

We don't say anything for a while again, so I guess maybe the narrator's got writer's block or something and then a great big skinhead dude tries to carjack us, but I end up beating the shit out of him using my badass martial arts skills. I get back in the car after telling the guy not to quit his day job and we drive out of the garage towards the Marshall Wilkins Convention Center.

"What was that all about then?" Jenny asks as we merge back onto the highway. "That guy has nothing to do with the Church of Solarism or the Fuerst Brothers or the sci-fantasy books their father wrote on their plane of existence, right?"

"Chandler's Law." I roll down the window and spit out a toothpick that the narrator lazily put in my mouth to make me look tough, which is a trope I never really understood to be honest. "When in doubt, have a man come through a door with a gun in his hand."

"Well done," that British voice actor asshole says after the magic tablet blasts our car stereo with another energy beam. "And speaking of guns…"

CHAPTER XXII

Danny Hanson's steady hand gently gripped his rifle, the small target before him squarely between the crosshairs of his scope. After exhaling the stale air which had occupied his lungs for what seemed like forever, Hanson squeezed the trigger and a .22-calibre bullet blasted forward, traveling exactly one hundred yards before striking the very center of his target.

His commanding officer watching closely, Hanson received a reluctant round of applause from his fellow snipers. His victory in the First Annual United Aryan Front Sharpshooting Contest was now complete.

"Congratulations Hanson," Lieutenant Thomas Rogers said, patting the young soldier on the shoulder.

"Thank you, Sir," Hanson said forcefully, his chiseled jaw facing north in a proud, noble manner as his light blonde hair fluttered ever-so-slightly at the behest of a stiff breeze which was coming in from the east.

"Come with me, Mann," Rogers said, motioning for the young marksman to follow him.

Lieutenant Rogers led Hanson into a nearby tent in which several other high-ranking UAF officers were huddled around a table, leafing through maps and offi-

BRYCE ALLEN

cial-looking documents. They paid no attention to Rogers and Hanson as they entered the aluminum-framed shelter.

"Son, winning this tournament affords you more than you think... You don't just get a ribbon for coming in first, understand?" Rogers asked.

"No, Sir, I'm afraid I don't," Hanson replied.

Rogers walked over to the table around which sat the now-silent group of commanding officers. They watched intently as the lieutenant picked up a manila envelope and carried it, formally, back over to Hanson[70].

"You haven't been with our outfit long, Hanson. But your marksmanship is incredibly well-developed."

"Thank you, sir, I did compete on my college shooting team back in Utah... National champs my junior year."

"Right, well, regardless—having proven yourself as the best sniper in this particular unit you will be charged with a very... *special* mission, Mann."

Rogers handed Hanson the thick, tightly-packed envelope. The plan to conscript an Olympic-caliber sniper into the United Aryan Front had worked out perfectly. Unscrupulous drama teachers, unsuspecting agents, and a remarkably impressionable, easily-manipulated recruit from Utah had led to this moment—the starting point for Operation Tacticus, Heinrich Fuerst's magnum opus.

Lieutenant Rogers wiped his thick, sloping brow with the back of his hand and continued. "Son, in that package you'll find a set of instructions as well as some falsified

---

[70] From Wikipedia: Pronunciation of lieutenant is generally split between the forms lef-ten-ənt and luːˈtɛnənt, with the former generally associated with the armies of the United Kingdom and Commonwealth countries, and the latter generally associated with anyone from the United States.

181

identification papers... Everything you'll need for this particular mission."

Hanson looked through the brightly-colored documents quickly, finding a security badge and building layout for the Marshall Wilkins Convention Center, a street map of Los Angeles, a hotel reservation sheet, and a glossy photograph of Gary Thompson–President of the United States.

"What's this Sir?" Hanson asked, holding up the president's glossy eight-by-ten.

"That's your target Son. It's all explained in that package, don't worry."

Hanson's brainwashed, decidedly unintelligent mind didn't think twice about the enormity of the duty he was being charged with. He was numb to almost everything now, the result of an intensified administration of The Treatment by the UAF's westernmost division.

"When is this mission to be carried out, Sir?"

"Like I said, Hanson, it's all in the package you have there... Obermann Smith will escort you personally to your hotel and arrange for your entrance into the convention center. Your weapon will already be in place, all you have to worry about is hitting your target."

Billy Joe Smith entered the tent just as Rogers finished speaking, giving an enthusiastic Nazi salute as he stood next to Hanson and faced his Lieutenant.

Originally from a trailer park somewhere in Arkansas, Smith had moved to California in his mid-teens to become a Hollywood stunt man. He'd been inspired by a popular television program whose 'stars' performed violent, ridiculous acts which often left them hospitalized. A naturally athletic, fearless young man, Smith had nonetheless been frustratingly unable to find steady work as a stuntman upon arriving in L.A. After being fired from a series of menial jobs he had fallen into a life of destitution when he had encountered a recruitment officer for the Church of Solarism, which had recently started targeting wannabes from other sections of the entertainment industry.

After joining the church and being assigned to the UAF's militant faction, Billy Joe had risen through the ranks quickly despite being given only a diluted dosage of The Treatment. The son of a fourth-generation Klansman, Smith had been exposed to brutal domestic violence and racist tirades throughout his childhood. The Treatment had been successful in weaning Smith off drugs—crystal meth to be precise—however, and his lucid, sharp mind took to the United Aryan Front's ethos like a duck to water[71].

Now, the dutiful Obermann was charged with completing the most important mission in the UAF's history—delivering Danny Hanson to a podium from which he would conduct the opening overture of a symphony of destruction which was to set the stage for a dynastic millennium of Aryan glory.

"You're in good hands, Hanson—Billy Joe here is the best damn soldier we have."

"Thank you, Sir, I'm confident that this mission will be successful," Obermann Smith replied with unnecessary

---

[71] idiom [id-ee-uh m], noun.
An expression whose meaning is not predictable from the usual meanings of its constituent elements, as kick the bucket or hang one's head, or from the general grammatical rules of a language, as the table round for the round table, and that is not a constituent of a larger expression of like characteristics.

loudness, shaking the limp hand of a vacant Danny Hanson. "It's nice to meet you, Hanson. I've heard great things about your marksmanship."

Grinning diabolically, Lieutenant Rogers slapped both men facing him on the shoulder, nodding approvingly as he said, in his thick southern twang: "This is just fantastic, Boys—I'm sure you two will get along great on this here mission. You'd best be on your way now—all gassed up, Obermann?"

"Yes Sir, we'll be in Los Angeles by eleven hundred hours on the morrow, giving us plenty of time to ready for the operation."

"That's great Son, you be sure to explain everything to Hanson on your trip. This is his first mission for us y'know."

"I won't let you down, Sir," Hanson stated, blankly.

Smith grabbed Hanson by the arm and walked him out of the tent as Rogers turned back to face his fellow UAF officers.

"You think your boy can get this done, Lieutenant?" Colonel Stan Stevens asked, his booming, cigar chomping voice offering a hint of doubt.

"Absolutely," Rogers replied, confidently. "Smith has never let us down before, Colonel, and I don't foresee any difficulties in escorting an unarmed halfwit into a sizeable convention center… Their papers and such are all in order, everything should go smoothly as far as I can see."

"And the weapon is already hidden in one of the luxury suites?" asked Brigadeführer Dustin Vinyard, a harsh-looking man in his forties whose notoriously short temper, freshly-shaven bald head, and well-kept Van Dyck beard made him easily the most intimidating figure on the base at the moment.

"Yes, Brigadeführer, the four pieces of the rifle were hidden in four separate compartments of the suite several weeks ago by our inside man at the convention center," said Rogers. "He is the head engineer at the building and will be joining the governor's security team during the pre-speech inspection. Obermann Smith will be carrying the scope with him, disguised as a pair of binoculars obviously."

"And should this... Hanson... be unable to get into position to take the shot?" Vinyard asked.

"Obermann Smith has brought a ceramic pistol with him in case of emergency... Should Mann Hanson be unable to reach his destination, he has been instructed to... improvise."

《《—》》

"So those are the guys we've got to stop at this thing?" I ask the British guy reading to us. "Hanson and Smith?"

"Maybe," he tells me through the tinny Jap-made speakers. "Maybe not."

"Which is it, asshole?"

"Cheerio," the Lymie says as we make a sharp turn onto a decrepit city street and the stereo starts to short circuit, spitting out some bright sparks and shit that don't really cause any problems for us but Jenny screams and hits the thing with her shoe which cures its electronic seizure and causes a drone-like whimper to emanate from the speakers for a few seconds. Then the steering wheel stops obeying my prehensile commands and the car drives itself to a nearby public tennis court and spends way too much time watching a bizarre match take place[72].

<<<—>>>

"The Marshall Wilkins Convention Center originally opened in 1991, its completion having been drastically delayed by an earthquake two years earlier that had affected much of California and reduced a near-complete civic auditorium to a pile of broken rubble.

"When it was finally completed, the convention center had cost taxpayers nearly triple its original estimated price, and was widely considered an architectural eyesore to boot.

"Largely playing host to entertainers whose popularity was either waning or about to disappear altogether, scoring the president's impending speech had been a major coup for Bill Hagan, the MWCC's operations director, who had been mired in a mid-career slump for several months before earning accolades galore from the venue's board of directors by managing to lure the prestigious event away from bigger arenas such as the majestic Badgley Hall."

I thank SUZI for the info and shut down my smartphone as we pull into a parking lot a mile-and-a-half from the venue and squeeze into a spot between a pair of ACME-brand rocket-powered motorscooters.

"Well, going by the Theory of Narrative Causality... I should be able to get us a pair of tickets pretty easily here," I tell Jenny, who stares back at me absently. There's an elderly couple wearing matching maroon THOMPSON FOR PREZ sweatshirts

[72] The tennis this group of individuals is playing appears to be a team-based competition of some kind. There's a map of the world drawn in chalk across three courts and a half-dozen teenagers are lobbing balls at one another, the backs of their shirts emblazoned with strange words that I don't recognize even though I speak like 20 languages now.

up ahead, so I approach them and claim to be with the LAPD, quickly flashing them my wallet which in no way, shape or form contains anything that remotely resembles a police badge. "Several counterfeit tickets have been circulating for this event," I tell them. "May I see your tickets, Sir?" I hold out my hand and the old man looks cautiously at his wife for a minute before reaching into his back pocket and pulling out two small rectangular pieces of cardboard adorned with small holograms. I give them a cursory glance and tell them they're phonies and I'll have to confiscate them for evidence and the guy starts to protest but his old lady hits him with her purse and tells him to shut up and that the whole thing is his fault for buying the tickets from some idiot friend of his. The octogenarians skulk away, their argument continuing unabated.

"Pretty slick there... Slick," Jenny says as she catches up to me. I thank her for the compliment and go to hand her one of the tickets but then there's a sudden flash of light and she's gone. I look down and see a little green globule on the ground where she'd been standing[73].

«‹‹—››»

Security is suspiciously light for a presidential appearance[74]. The metal detectors look like they're on loan from a local high

---

[73] From Wikipedia: Spontaneous human combustion (SHC) is a term encompassing reported cases of the combustion of a living (or very recently deceased) human body without an apparent external source of ignition. In addition to reported cases, examples of SHC appear in literature, and both types have been observed to share common characteristics regarding circumstances and remains of the victim.

[74] From AllTheTropes.Wikia.com: 'Swiss Cheese Security' - Characters can enter the premises whenever the plot necessitates it, despite presumably locked doors or obvious obstacles. Any trouble they should logically run into seems to be deliberately not shown. Sometimes this is just a matter of not having enough money for a transitional set.

187

school and the Secret Service guys all look out-of-shape and disinterested as fuck. I make my way through the checkpoints quickly, no sign of potential snipers anywhere amidst the zealous horde of Thompson supporters.

A fat millennial chick bumps into me and doesn't apologize so I call her a bunch of awful names, but they don't really register since she's staring at her smartphone and humming a showtune-like melody that I can't quite place. Just when I'm about to launch a fresh round of insults at this broad, I spot another female a couple hundred yards ahead of us that I'm pretty sure is my daughter.

«‹——›»»

Iris is with a couple of shady-looking dudes who are almost certainly—based on Bellisario's Maxim—the spotter and shooter that the Solarites sent to take out Thompson. I can't quite figure out why Iris is with them, but I guess maybe they think it makes them blend in better having a young girl with them and such? Sure, let's go with that.

I follow Iris and her pals as they make their way up to the second level of the auditorium, slowly but surely closing in on them. One of the guys catches me looking at them and we exchange a Meaningful Look, both of us squinting menacingly as if we're about to reach for our six shooters at high noon.

The trio presses on and I begin to get aggressive in making my way through the crowd. Iris and I lock eyes briefly, but she doesn't seem to recognize me, which is a bitch. I guess she's been brainwashed and shit though so that adds up. Totally.

A super tall ginger with bad teeth cuts in front of me so I get into it with him for a hot minute and by the time we're done arguing about who the bigger asshole is – he's *literally* a big asshole but whatever – I've completely lost track of my daughter and her crew. Fuck. I assume that time is of the essence, so I ask the narrator to disobey the Law of Conservation of Detail, pull a Diabolus ex Machina out of his ass and give me psychic clairvoyance for a minute so I can know where they went and he readily agrees[75].

《《──》》

In a whirlwind of motions Bishop bursts into the storage room on the upper concourse at the convention center and catches his daughter and her cohorts assembling a graphite rifle of some kind with tools they'd smuggled through security. The two male members of the Church of Solarism immediately descend upon our 'hero' and try to subdue him with some elementary wrestling holds but he eludes them easily prior to rendering both men unconscious with a pair of lightning-fast haymakers to the jaw.

"Let's go," Bishop says, turning to face his frightened daughter.

"Who are you?" she asks, backing into a rickety wooden shelving unit that really shouldn't be there for a variety of reasons. "Who sent you?"

"Jesus, what the hell did they do to you, Kiddo?" Bishop slowly steps forward, holding his hands up in front of him to imply his peaceful intentions. "It's me. I'm your father. I'm here to help, to save you."

Iris gasps and starts to cry as her pre-cult memories begin to take shape in her brain. She crouches down against the curiously-stationed shelving unit and nudges it enough to cause a full paint can to fall from its perch, knocking her out cold…

《《──》》

---

[75] ¯_(ツ)_/¯

No one blinks an eye when I walk through the convention center with an unconscious dame slung over my shoulder, but then I hear a couple of gunshots ring out and a shit ton of screaming as we reach the exit, so I guess those Solarites I punched out regained consciousness.

Absolute bedlam ensues and a hurricane of pandemonium swiftly courses through the arena, somehow propelling us forward through the onslaught of cops and first responders arriving on the scene, wholly unconcerned with me or my lifeless daughter. We make our way back to the parking lot and manage to drive away without being stopped by anyone.

Iris is still comatose when we get back to the motel, so I tuck her in bed and grab a seat on the semi-putrid sofa they stuffed in here at some point in the seventies and watch the news for a little while. Apparently, Thompson survived the assassination attempt and the shooter and his accomplice committed suicide by cyanide tablet before they could be questioned. A young woman was seen with them earlier in the day and is now being sought for questioning. Every channel is pretty much saying the exact same shit over and over again. I glance over at the magic tablet on the dresser and think about firing it up, but then my daughter wakes up, so I don't.

Iris asks me where she is. I fill her in and she tells me to take her back to the Silver Station immediately.

"You realize you're a person of interest in a major national news story, right?" I ask her.

She looks at me like I'm crazy (well… whatever.) so I turn the TV back on to show her the news coverage of the assassination attempt but WAVEFRONT is on every channel at the exact same spot, which I'm pretty sure is early on in the story, exactly where the last clip we endured ended actually…

EXT. MAIN DECK OF THE NEPTUNE. BADYN EMERGES
FROM BELOW AND MAKES HIS WAY OVER TO A
MIDDLE-AGED, FORMAL LOOKING MAN AND A BEAU-
TIFUL YOUNG WOMAN DISCUSSING THE CONTENTS OF
A DIGITAL MAP. THIS IS SHIP CAPTAIN CADEYRN
AARIS AND HIS DAUGHTER FLAVIA.

          BADYN
    Good morning, captain, have
    you determined how close we
    are to the edge of the
    world yet?

          CADEYRN
    Badyn. Glad to see you've
    finally found your sea
    legs.

          BADYN
    I have! Only a week into
    this journey to oblivion as
    well.

IDOL THREAT

CADEYRN
Your sentiments regarding
this venture have been well-
documented, hoplite. As have
those of ninety percent of
the men and women aboard
this vessel. That does not
change the fact that we're
headed for the northern
banks of Kenortia.

BADYN
Right, around the top of
the world… Which you claim
to be round.

FLAVIA
It *is* round, aditu! The
worlds in the sky, the
moon, the sun—they are all
round, it only stands to
reason that our planet is
the same.

CADEYRN
Badyn Taylor, this is my
daughter—Flavia.

 BADYN
Your reputation precedes
you, Miss Aaris. HE SHAKES
HER HAND. The sales job you
did on the Grand Council
isn't liable to work on me
though.

 FLAVIA
Well it's a good thing
you're not important enough
to make high-level deci-
sions regarding the fate of
the dominion, Mr. Taylor.

 BADYN
Ha, well that's probably
true.

 CADEYRN
Prandeast is being served
on the other side of the
ship, Badyn.

BADYN
Thank you, sir, I suppose I
could stand a little suste-
nance this morning. I
wouldn't want to meet the
afterlife on an empty
stomach. Very nice to meet
you, Ms. Aaris.

FLAVIA
Good day, Mr. Taylor.

CADEYRN
Enjoy your meal, slugger.

Badyn walks away. Flavia watches him
leave, a hint of curiosity in her eyes.

EXT. OTHER SIDE OF THE SHIP; BADYN
APPROACHES A LARGE OUTDOOR MEAL HALL AREA
WITH 1-2 DOZEN SOLDIERS EATING. HE GRABS A
LARGE WOODEN BOWL AT THE END OF A LENGTHY
TABLE AND MAKES HIS WAY DOWN A PROCESSION
OF BUFFET-STYLE FOOD DISPENSERS. A YOUNG
COOK APPROACHES HIM, QUITE OBVIOUSLY AN
EXCITED STREAMBALL FAN.

COOK
Morning, Badyn! Get any
sleep in that storm last
night?

BADYN
Managed to count a few
appena, how about you?

COOK
Yeah yeah, I mean… Well, I
didn't get much sleep but
at least we didn't sink,
right?!

BADYN
(finishes stocking his bowl)
Yeah, that's always nice.
Take it easy, kid.

COOK
Thanks, Badyn, you too!

Badyn takes a seat at a table with a
group of soldiers, who glare at him
uneasily.

>   BADYN
> You boys mind if I sit with
> you?

A bearded man about the same size as
Badyn is looked to by his peers. He
continues to eat, without looking up at
Badyn. This is CYNBEL, veteran soldier
and de facto leader of the ship's
infantrymen.

>   CYNBEL
> Sure thing, superstar.

>   BADYN
>   Thanks.

HE BEGINS TO EAT.

>   SOLDIER #3
> I was at that game against
> the New Tyre last season
> where you scored four
> caedos, Mr. Taylor. You're
> the best euzon in the
> league as far as I'm
> concerned.

Badyn reaches over and shakes the fan's hand.

                    BADYN
        Thanks very much. Hopefully
        you'll get to see me score
        a few more when this war is
        over with.

                    CYNBEL
        You must've done something
        pretty bad to get shipped
        out with the likes of us,
        superstar.

                    BADYN
        I volunteered, amica.
        Wanted to do my part to
        help the dominion.

                    SOLDIER #3
        It's true, sir—I saw a
        digitron report on it,
        Badyn signed up, walked
        away from his RSL contract
        and everything.

                CYNBEL
That's what the news
ministry told us, satum,
not what actually happened.
They got a lot of mileage
out of this simia volun-
teering—so many kids signed
up afterwards they didn't
have to go through with
plans to expand conscrip-
tion.

                BADYN
You must be a Peltasts fan,
huh culus?

                CYNBEL
(standing up to leave table)
Never really had much time
for streamball, too busy
doing a real man's job in
the mines. BADYN GLOWERS AT
CYNBEL. You gonna join us
for drills this afternoon,
superstar? Now that we've
all got our sea legs the
brass wants us to start
preparing for the invasion.

I'll be leading a demon-
stration on hand-to-hand
combat, would love for you
to see how a *real* gladiator does things.

BADYN
Wouldn't miss it for the
world… Superstar.

Sorry for that… Anyway, so then Badyn goes on to beat the shit out of Cynbel in the demonstration obviously but then he gets in trouble for it because of military protocol or whatever and they say more gay-sounding shit that no viewer can possibly understand. The guy playing Badyn I recognize from that talking baby movie in the '80s and a few of the other actors look familiar as well but the movie definitely sucks. At any rate, Iris is totally transfixed by the thing—hypnotized really—and doesn't respond to anything I do to try and break her from the trance and I can't turn off the TV, even when I unplug it, so I grab the tablet to see if I can figure out what the Solarites might be up to next, so I can track them down and maybe get the cure for that brainwashing potion they infected my daughter with…

CHAPTER XXIII

Gary Thompson was the rarest of prominent politicians—the kind that had little concern for leaving a 'legacy' or an 'imprint on history'. He possessed a genuine, unwavering love for his country that had captivated voters, and helped him win one of the most lopsided presidential elections in American history. A distinguished-looking, modestly handsome man in his mid-fifties, Thompson had never forgotten his humble beginnings as a school teacher in Wyoming, always placing an emphasis on education and affordable daycare from his first term as Mayor of Cheyenne to his dozen years in the Senate to his triumphant rise to the oval office.

His campaign slogan had been profound in its simplicity—'U.S. = US'—and the first two-and-half years of Thompson's presidency had been largely based upon justifying the belief he had wrangled from all walks of life for a brief period during an electoral year. 'Catching lightning in a bottle always ends up burning your hands' his extremely vocal right-wing detractors would often quip, eagerly waiting for him to plummet in the polls.

The assignation attempt in California had troubled the president greatly—almost as much as the scandal his close friend and former Vice President was forced to endure in the preceding weeks. Thompson was definitely glad to have left the month of June behind him, the most trying thirty-day stretch any sitting Commander in Chief had been forced to contend with in recent memory. With his popularity waning and the conservatives rallying around an upstart Congressman from Michigan in anticipation of the next election, Thompson was unable to take a much-needed leave of absence from the political arena however, his cross-country barnstorming tour set to continue out of a necessity now flirting with premature desperation.

The united left was unwilling to allow their opponents to gather any further ammunition in anticipation of a multi-year battle on Capitol Hill. By not allowing a Vice Presidential resignation or an assassination attempt to interrupt their fearless leader's trek through nearly every major American city, the liberals believed they were demonstrating an unequivocal sense of courage that would go a long way towards earning Thompson a second term in office.

Wolfgang Fuerst had been the logical choice to succeed Carl Mason as V.P. A unifying figure with ties to both major parties, the incredibly popular ex-actor had given Thompson's approval rating a significant boost when the announcement had been made.

Members of Thompson's staff were still bringing Fuerst up to speed on a variety of issues back in Washington as Thomson readied to board the presidential helicopter in Tucson. Thousands of Mexican immigrants had fawned over the man who had famously passed the historic Immigration Reform Bill in his first 100 Days during his brief stay in the border town, giving the president's badly-bruised ego a much-needed lift.

Thompson was to travel by helicopter up to Phoenix where a private jet was waiting to fly him back to Washington in anticipation of a grandiose parade on Independence Day, an event that would also serve as Vice President Fuerst's first official joint appearance with the 'Champion of the Underprivileged'.

The president shuddered as he thought of the pose his press secretary would insist on as he and Fuerst held their first joint press conference together—the two men facing each other with their fists in the air playfully as if they were to adorn a poster promoting an upcoming boxing match. *Just part of the game… Play it up for all its worth.*

As his limousine pulled up next to a massive helicopter, Thompson thought back to his first months as Commander in Chief—a simpler time that had preceded so much turmoil. He grinned timorously as one of the secret service agents most familiar to him ushered the president from his car towards the chopper.

"Have a safe flight Mr. President, we'll see you on the ground in Phoenix!" Bruce Sherrill, his most senior body-guard, shouted beneath the deafening sound of the helicopter's propeller.

"Thanks Bruce—try not to get pulled over for speeding on your way up there, Arizona's governor is a huge jerk!" the president replied, his last words being muffled by the sound of the hydraulic door above him springing to life and closing in a coldly efficient manner, enclosing Thompson in the most expensive rotary-wing aircraft ever built.

Thompson thought for a moment that something had seemed different about Bruce somehow—his voice perhaps? Maybe a new hair cut? Something? Anything? *Your mind's playing tricks on you...*

An engineering marvel, the vessel dubbed 'The Flying Tank' by the press had been completed only a few weeks earlier and was seemingly encased with as much armor as a hundred-ton battleship. The bulky helicopter was impervious to most any external attack, and the president's security team was insistent that he travel in it during intercity trips in the wake of the frightening incident at the Marshall Wilkins Convention Center which was still under investigation.

Sighing gently and sinking into the extra-wide, beige leather seat that comprised the entirety of the rotorcraft's interior, Thompson reached for a copy of *Here & Now* magazine—a guilty pleasure of his since his Senatorial days—as The Flying Tank began its ascent into the blue Arizona sky.

Thirty seconds later, a brilliant ball of orange fire erupted from beneath Thompson's chair, a churning heap of twisted metal soon lying on the ground below. The vessel's pilot and the lone passenger aboard had both been incinerated.

The only clue of any kind investigators recovered from the wreckage was a copper medallion that survived the horrific crash miraculously unscathed. Engraved upon either side of the modest pendant were Shahar—the Carthaginian God of Dawn—and Shapash, the once-powerful Western Mediterranean nation's Sun Goddess.

《《《—》》》

I notice that there's a fuzzy glow around everything in the room now and an old-fashioned clock on the wall I never noticed before is spinning around super-fast, so I guess we're jumping ahead in time in both stories since everything's been synched up for a while now. I speed-read through a couple of chapters while still half-paying attention to the movie and Iris remains zombified. After Thompson's killed and Wolf becomes president his evil brother gives a big evil speech and then the Solarites stage a bunch of terrorist attacks across the country that fuck up a bunch of cities royally so that the Fuersts can have an excuse to pass emergency measures that give the executive branch all kinds of extra powers that can let them start turning the U.S. into the Fourth Reich, which I guess is a pretty good plan under the circumstances. They even make sure it's a Christian terrorist group that gets blamed so that Solarism can seem less crazy and start to become the country's main religion. Diabolical! There's also a chapter about a side deal Heinrich strikes with a bigtime pharmaceutical company to let them provide the placebo to the fake poison they're going to pretend is in a bunch of cities' water supplies which I think has some social commentary undertones but who really cares at this point? Iris mumbles something about waffles and the clock on the wall slows down just as the glow around everything fades and we're back on the regular timeline. That stupid movie is still playing somehow but then it gets interrupted for a special message from the oval office...

CHAPTER XXIV

An expensive-looking camera sat perfectly still atop an expensive-looking tripod as President Fuerst pretended to fervently study the notes that the FBI had given him only moments earlier.

Wolfgang had never used cue cards during his tenure as the world's top action movie star, and he had likewise refused to rely upon a teleprompter throughout his decade-long political career. On this occasion however, he had agreed to have his words spoon-fed to him, fearful that anything might be out of place as he addressed a nation suddenly hemorrhaging pride, crippled by fear...

The hulking Baby Boomer calmly collected his thoughts, getting into character as he'd done hundreds of times before—this time to deliver what would be the performance of his career.

Taking a generous gulp of water from a carefully situated glass which sat atop his new desk, Wolf folded the notes he'd been given in half, storing them in the top drawer of the last remnant of the HMS Resolute.

The iconic desk, which had originally been presented to President Hayes in 1880 by Queen Victoria as a token of friendship between England and the United States, looked almost absurd in its attempt to house the broad-shouldered Austrian immigrant.

"Let's do this, Teddy," Fuerst said in a melodic growl, his voice booming with resonant conceit.

Only a few members of the presidential staff looked on as the White House Press Secretary instructed the cameraman to begin, pointing at Wolfgang and nodding his head purposefully as he dissolved into the background.

Taking a deep breath, Wolfgang began.

"My fellow Americans," he said, affecting a dramatic, stouthearted inflection.

"I am not here tonight to recount the horrors of what has transpired on this most tragic of days… Today's date will undoubtedly go down in the annals of history as one of the darkest days in human existence… Words cannot begin to express the shock… the outrage… the anger… that I, and all of you, have felt as we've witnessed these acts of cowardly terrorism being carried out upon cities… upon citizens… of this still-great country. The most egregious aspect of this sickening tragedy is that it seems that some of our own people—Americans—are responsible for the attacks… A fanatical religious organization known as Christ Fire has claimed responsibility for the terrorist acts that were carried out in no fewer than fourteen American cities today… Acts so despicable and so abhorrent that I cannot bring myself to offer any adequate description of them…[76]"

Wolf paused for dramatic effect, coughing in a manner which convincingly suggested that he was becoming overwhelmed with emotion.

---

[76] They were really really bad though. Fo' reals. Pittsburgh got it the worst — sorry, Pittsburgh!

The president continued.

"While I wish I could tell you now that those responsible for the events of July 11 are right now in custody, sadly, I cannot… Indeed, it seems that the threat posed by Christ Fire is greater than we ever dreamed possible, and this nightmare of national security appears poised to continue… In a letter sent to the FBI, Christ Fire claims to have poisoned several major metropolitan areas' water supplies with a deadly, undetectable poison known as Thaylex Four that will begin taking effect in the coming days."

As millions collectively held their breath in the wake of his last sentence, Wolf channeled his boxing persona and stared furiously, intently into the curved lens before him.

"But fear not… at this very moment government agencies from coast to coast are working with chemistry firms and production centers to both create and distribute the antidote to Thaylex Four in time to avoid any further deaths at the hands of Christ Fire… Please stay tuned to your local news networks and the official White House Chirrup and ChumSpot feeds for further information on where and when your city will be administering the antidote. Rest assured, I've been told that within twenty-four hours this remedy will be produced in sufficient quantity so as to supply the entire country… I compel you to not panic, and to follow the guidelines for receiving the antidote in an orderly fashion. We must now, more than ever, band together under a banner of courage as we seek to defeat this extreme threat which has manifested itself within our very borders…"

Readying for the final phase of his speech, Wolf again took a drink of water from his monarchial chalice.

"Tomorrow I will go before Congress and request emergency executive powers so as to deal with this evil organization firmly and immediately. While my first week in office has been incredibly trying, I am now, more than ever, dedicated to preserving America's safety... To do this, I will require the full cooperation of all of our leaders, and I promise you right here and now that those responsible for 7/11 will be brought to justice, and that order will be restored to this country which has given us all so much... Lady Liberty has been a generous mother to us all... Now we must pay her back through an unerring faith in her greatness... Even if faith in God, perverted as it may be, has seemingly led to this monumental disaster, we must keep our faith in our nation intact... With the powers I expect Congress to bestow upon me, I will be able to do all that is necessary to capture Christ Fire's leaders and bring an end to the madness that they have created through their unthinkable acts of violence."

Heinrich entered the room, grinning maliciously while his brother executed the brilliant speech he'd written flawlessly—a truly award-caliber performance. *Everything thus far has gone exactly according to plan, without a hitch... Validation shall soon be mine, our oath fulfilled at my behest!*

"I leave you tonight with a promise, America... I promise to make it my mission to restore order... to restore justice... to restore honor to this country that I love so very much... This is a job I wish did not have to be done, but one that I will accomplish with both urgency and vitality..."

Heinrich motioned for Wolf to wrap it up, twirling his right hand in a clockwise manner, his eyebrows raised tellingly.

"While I must now leave you in this broadcast, know that I will never leave you in spirit… This is our darkest hour America, but I vow to you that the impending dawn will indeed be bright… The power of the sun is already beckoning, as we are now united as a single force–a powerful ambition bellowing within all of us… To exact justice upon Christ Fire and all those who have aided them in their crusade of evil… Good night, America. Rest well knowing that you will be safe as the sun rises on another day–a day which beckons with the promise of redemption."

Press Secretary Conrad held his right hand up in a fist, the red light atop the camera going dim as the caustic, usually-emotionless men in the room wiped away tears and clapped loudly.

Wolfgang stood and bowed gently, retrieving the FBI's notes from the Resolute Desk and shaking several hands prior to retiring to the Lincoln Bedroom where a lingerie-clad Leslie McKay was waiting.

Henry Krauss, the president's mysterious 'advisor', stayed up all night, plotting how he might best usurp the throne now that Operation Tacticus had been successfully carried out. *Patience Heinrich, your time will come… Soon enough.*

《《———》》

Iris seems like she's starting to regain her lucidity. I start reciting a nursery rhyme her mom used to sing to her when she was a baby but then the magic tablet shoots out a blinding orange light that digitizes me and sucks me into its world. A cohort of Rodinian guards arrest me as soon as I fall from the sky into a lake they're resting near and take me back to the capital where I'm put on trial in the King's Court for being a Nadiri spy or some shit but when I tell them my name the King remembers that I once wired him a thousand bucks to help get him back in power, which it looks like he did, so then he pardons me and instructs his chief magic guy to send me back to my own dimension.

The Rodinian sorcerer looks a LOT like the Russian wizard who sold me the magic tablet back at the start of the book, so I ask him if he has any relatives back where I'm from and it turns out their cousins. Small Multiverse. A human-sized dragon asks me if I've seen his nephew in my realm by any chance, but I just shrug and play dumb. Pretty sure he buys it.

Before I get teleported away I ask the Sorcerer Supreme if there's anything he can give me to help me take down the Fuerst brothers once I'm back home. He smiles wryly and tells me that tampering with mystic interdimensional forces can be dangerous but then he laughs and conjures up an invisibility cloak, two wooden beakers filled with a time-traveling potion and a magic sword that he says will serve me well in my quest. I take the items and thank the dude before he zaps me in the head with his enchanted wand and tells me that he's also enhanced my Dexterity (DEX), Wisdom (WIS) and Charisma (CHR) levels exponentially. So now I've got that going for me. Which is nice.

«« —»»

Iris is back in her catatonic state when I get back to the motel room after I take a bus out to the west coast from the random Midwestern town that Rodinia's Sorcerer Supreme teleported me to. I turn on the TV. It's showing news footage of the military's standoff with Christ Fire soldiers at their compound in Texas and when I turn the magic tablet back on and carefully load up LiveStory, issuing a formal warning to the thing for it not to zap me back into that other dimension again, the prose on the app is again matching up perfectly with the live news, complete with cadence emphasis and caesuras and such. I chug one of the time-travel potion beakers and start to dissolve as I skip ahead to the last couple of pages, which take place in the Year of the Super Budget Discount Rewards Club...

EPILOGUE

WOLFGANG FUERST lay motionless within a thick glass case, a full-time taxidermist always on call to tend to his perfectly-preserved, mannequin-like corpse.

On the eve of the twentieth anniversary of the Solarite Rising, his tomb would soon be paid homage to by the entirety of the High Council. Archbaron Krauss himself, now well into his ninth decade of life, would also be making a brief visit to the tomb, although his waning health likely meant that the media and adoring masses would be kept at bay as he paid respects to his late brother.

Laura Krauss, Heinrich's most recent wife, was in New York, overseeing the grandiose parade taking place to honor the special day.

Malcolm Gilmour was getting ready to host a prime-time television special on SOL1, showcasing the Federation's first twenty years of glory starting with the commercial-free broadcast of his cinematic masterpiece *The Art of Triumph*. Declan Farrelly, meanwhile, was still on a diplomatic mission in New Europe, serving as an advisor during the negotiations of the Treaty of Toulon.

Heinrich instructed his body guards to stand down as he slowly made his way towards his brother's tomb. He stopped a few inches from the case, slowly lowering his head towards Wolfgang's empty life vessel.

Whispering in an unholy rasp, Heinrich began speaking to the revered corpse of a being with whom he'd one shared a womb.

"The High Council plots against me, Brother, I can sense it..." A demented, increasingly violent sense of paranoia had overtaken the Archbaron at some point during his fifteenth year of reign over the Western Federation. He now spoke in delusional, irrational sentence fragments as his mental health was further along in the deterioration process than anyone close to him would care to admit.

The irony of discussing a nonexistent assassination plot against him with the brother he had himself murdered years earlier managed to elude Heinrich as he rambled on semi-coherently for nearly twenty minutes.

At long last Krauss grew weary of the one-sided conversation he'd been having. He turned back towards the heavily-guarded entrance of the monumental temple which housed the preserved corpse of the deified martyr who had heroically founded the Continental Republic, the Federation's immediate predecessor, from the ruinous ashes of the United States of America.

Stumbling back towards the retinue surrounding his armored limousine, Heinrich quickly glimpsed up at the sky, humbled for the first time in years as at that exact moment the moon was crossing the sun, a brilliant eclipse beaming from the heavens in breathtaking fashion. The celestial collision soon emitted a blinding flash of light that hurled a glowing neon orb towards the earth...

IDOL THREAT

Fuerst/Krauss' guards begin shooting at me as soon as I land on the ground and the orb thingy I'm in explodes after breaking my fall. Sword in hand, I do a badass barrel roll towards the front of the temple and then I pull on my invisibility cloak and run away as they try to figure out what the hell is going on.

Then I go from guard to guard, impaling them each with my magic sword, which must look like it's operating on its own since I've still got the cloak on and all, until it's just me and Fuerst/Krauss left standing. I take the cloak off, for dramatic effect, and introduce myself as Shane Bishop – Tyrant Slayer, which is the coolest-sounding thing I can think of at the moment.

The old bastard mumbles something in German and then runs over to his limo. He pulls an old-looking spear out of his trunk and shouts out another Euro-sounding phrase as he hurls the thing at me.

I try to block the spear with my magic sword, but it goes right through the blade like it's nothing and pierces my stomach, so I guess it must have a higher weapon rating than the one I've got. I guess it's my fault for telling LiveStory to include it as a MacGuffin in the first place. Damn it. Fuerst/Krauss walks over to me as I fall to the ground and inspect my wound and tells me that I've just been impaled by the Spear of Destiny. He leans in to finish me off but I quickly down the second time-travel potion and grab hold of the Archbaron's leg just as another neon vortex opens and drag him back to the present.

《《—》》

214

Fuerst/Krauss curses me out when we crash land into the Oval Office and we both stagger to our feet as the younger versions of both Heinrich and Wolfgang stare at us, dumfounded. "Who the fuck are you?" Heinrich Prime asks as Wolfgang stands and instinctively adopts a boxer's stance. Both versions of Heinrich appear to recognize one another, and they start conversing in German at turbo speed. Wolfgang finally sees me bleeding and calls for medical attention as he rushes over to me. I whisper into his ear what the Epilogue told me and what I saw during my brief journey to the future and he thanks me as the EMS crew arrives along with a team of secret service guys.

President Fuerst instructs the medical personnel to get me to the hospital ASAP and then tells the scary-looking dudes in black suits to arrest both versions of Heinrich for Treason.

《《《——》》》

The second edition of IDOL THREAT I read while recovering in President Fuerst's personal hospital room after some world-class surgeons fix my wound up is a lot less entertaining than the original version, but Wolfgang gets to keep power at the end and goes on to do a lot of good things as Commander in Chief... So, I guess that's good. The magic tablet disintegrates after I finish reading the new version of the novel and it kinda burns my hands but not too bad.

Iris comes to see me as I'm being discharged and she's totally back to normal now, so I guess whatever spell the Solarites had her under is done with now that Heinrich's been taken care of and balance has been restored to the cosmos. It makes sense if you don't think about it.

IDOL THREAT

I take my daughter out for lunch and, against my better judgment, I order a PB & J sandwich which ends up being way better than the one I made in the opening chapter, thereby negating my earlier claims of its supremacy… Fuck.

THE END

Shane Bishop will return in IGNOBLE PURSUITS…

BRYCE ALLEN was born in Atlantic Canada in the early-1980s. He graduated from the University of King's College in 2004 with a BA in History and currently resides in the United States. His works include the cacographic anti-thrillers *The Spartak Trigger* and *Idol Threat*, both of which were published by Bedlam Press.

Made in the USA
Coppell, TX
16 December 2021

69071482R00120